CAUGHT
in a
storm

By Ali Marie

Book 1 of 2- Storm Series

To my mama, my best friend, my person. There is not a day you are not thought about nor a day you are not missed. I would sell my soul for more time with you because what I had is never enough. To the woman who built me up to who I am today. To the woman that gave me the best parts of her, that I fear the world never truly saw, but also gave me the romantic notion to love and stay through the hard times. To the woman who made me strong and independent. To the woman who gave me the superpower to push emotion aside as if it never existed to fight through life and all its demolishing moments. To you mama, who I know did the best job you could under all the circumstances you were handed in your life. I love and miss you more than an ocean filled with tears. This is for you, Mama ~

To Winston, my soulmate in a dark chocolate loyal English lab form. It has been two years without you, and you never leave my mind or heart. I miss my big snuggly pooh bear with all your antics and wisdom. No one knows how to indulge in ice cream and chick flick nights like you do. And no one else seems to care to bark and grunt at me if I am not in bed by a certain hour anymore. Or lay on top of me when my stress and anxiety is getting the best of me. You got me like no other and took all my secrets and wishes with you the day you passed. You loved my kids as if they were your own and greeted everyone that entered the house with a toy, blanket, or pillow. The stealer of food and also my heart, I love you. I hope you are getting so many cuddles and ear rubs with Mama. To my handsome old man, I am elated to have your personality shine throughout this book. Because everyone needs a Winston in their life.

Prologue: Emelia - 3 years ago

Half a minute. That was all I needed to get to her room before she took her last breath. As I walked down the hospital hallway, the nurse coming out of Mama's room stopped to stare at me. Only to hold the look of, *please do not let this be her daughter. This is not how I wanted to start my day.* Only for me to finally approach my mama's room, asking the nurse how she was today. "I am so sorry. She literally just took her last breath thirty seconds ago."

Taken back by her words, I could only stare at her, trying to get my mind wrapped around the fact she was gone, actually gone. It's not like this was not unexpected, as the outcome was exactly what was intended to happen, once she had made her decision. A decision that my sister and I could only support. The nurse let me know I can go in if I want, so I slowly pulled the handle and eerily walked into her hospital room. I honestly cannot say she looked peaceful, but I could feel a calming presence. Or maybe it was the lack of her presence that was disembarking on me.

I took out my cellphone to call my sister to let her know the dis-hearting news. We had hoped we had one more day at least. At least that was the hospice's guessing. She seemed to be just as taken back as I was with the news, but she is better than me at kicking her emotions down, to make sure things are taken care of. Letting her go to call the cremation company and make sure all other necessities are in order, I call the next person on my list, my fiancé. He lets me know he will be there shortly and hangs up, before I can tell him no.

Last, but not least, the one call I dreaded. My dad. He seemed to know as soon as he answered why I was calling first thing in the morning. As I find the words again to even say, "She's gone," he abruptly tells me, "I'll be up there in twenty minutes. Do not let them take her anywhere." Followed by hanging up on me.

All I could do was stand there, staring, as if I was willing her to somehow open her eyes and look at me. Tears refusing to fall, as doing so would be admitting that she was actually gone now. It would be acknowledging that my mama, my best friend is not a phone call away or an easy walk down the road to visit. The woman who was stronger than I ever gave her credit for and told me how it was, whether it was good or bad. She never tried to shelter her feelings from me, but instead tried to protect me from all the ugly of what she was going through in her marriage and health as best as she could. A nurse walked in, interrupting my thoughts. She finishes unhooking Mama from everything and getting ready to pull the sheet up over her head.

"NO!" I shout, then clear my throat, reigning in my emotions. "I mean no, sorry, please don't do that yet."

She nods then turns to leave. All the sudden panic arises in me that she does not look as peaceful as I would have thought. She has a frown on her face, and her hair is disheveled. Slowly walking up to the side of her bed, I realize I need to help make her look peaceful before my dad arrives. Slowly and very carefully, I turn her head to the right a little and start combing her hair down with my fingers. Based on the tangles, she might have had a slightly restless time as her body prepared itself for its final breath. I can only hope she was as comfortable with no pain as hospice had promised she would be with the IV of morphine. Slightly letting her head slowly fall back down to the pillow, I start combing through her hair on the right side. Feeling a presence, I turn around to see my fiancé standing at the door, staring at me in shock. Like I am playing with a corpse as if it was a Barbie doll's hair. Feeling the tenseness that he has brought in, I murmur, "You don't have to be here."

"I want to be here for you," he said as he continued to stare at me with concerned, questioning eyes.

"I need her to look peaceful before my dad gets here. I need to make sure she looks put together, like she is resting. Do not judge me right now… I know what I have to do."

Nothing left to say, he walks over, kisses me on the temple, and takes a seat on the couch by the window. I finish making my mama "presentable" for my dad then take a seat next to him on the couch. I can feel his whole body stiffen as he knows not what to say or do. Feeling him cringing that I touched my dead mother, I get up to wash my hands, thinking he cannot support me through this. I am not sure anyone can help me through the fact that she is really gone. Gone because decisions were made that there was no refuting. What good would that have done? She made her decision, and it was not my place to make her feel guilty about it or question her reasoning. I knew her reasoning. I lived through it, with it, bore witness to it. I head back over to sit in the chair next to Mama and stare at her with glossy eyes. Thinking, this moment, her face, those dying sounds, this past week is going to haunt me for the rest of my life.

Prologue 2: Lucas - a year ago

"You are such a wanker," my teammate yells out to me. "Well, you are a pompous angry little man of a twat. Stay the bloody hell out of my way. Especially on the damn track." Me, pushing six-four, Mario is barely five-six. "He is a stout mother fucker like an angry hobbit on steroids," I vent to Kent and my crew chief. "You need to keep him out of my way. Or the next time I will be slamming into him, not my brakes… Three positions I lost due to that tosser. Three!"

"You still finished in the top ten, mate," Henry spouts off.

"Not good enough. Top ten is never good enough. Needs to be top five at least, though I prefer first place. Top five is good enough for now. First is the ideal goal." Letting them take my rant in, the throwing of my gloves, my drink and whatever else I can get my hands on, before walking away. They are used to it. Should they be used to it? This was not how I planned to start the season, especially at Brands Hatch, which is more like a home base for me. Kent yells out to remind me we head out at six in the morning. Translation, no matter where my arse ends up tonight, it better be in the motorcoach by then.

I end up at one of the finer drinking institutions tonight. Giacomo, who drives for Lamborghini, sent a text to join him. He is my trusted wing man. Though we leave nothing to lose on the track; off the track we are a dynamite pair. Neither wants to change teams, but we love feeding the rumors of becoming teammates constantly. Tonight finds us at Blakes. Thirty minutes from the track, so not too far to travel knackered. Strolling into the club with my fitted Armani black pants and black belt with a gold buckle, suede derby shoes that are topped off with a white collared shirt that has sleeves rolled up. Finding Giacomo, he looks to be my twin in identical clothes with short sleek black hair and clean cut squared jawline, compared to my tousled dirty blonde hair with a slight scruff on my face. Slapping hands and pulling into our bro hug, he leans in so I can hear him over the loud thumping music. "So we have a bachelorette party to our right, a girl's night out in front of us, and a second bachelorette party to our left. Man, we are surrounded by hot drunk ladies tonight."

"Let's get a few drinks then and start making our rounds."

Hours later, multiple no, a trillion Goldschläger shots later, we are partying it up the dance floor with beautiful women. I have a gorgeous, tall blonde grinding against my hard-on, that if she does not stop soon, we may be in a predicament. G has three brunettes around him, and from the looks of it, they may be triplets, if not sisters. That is one lucky son of a bitch, but well deserved. He did win today, so let the man party it up and may this night lead to multiple women and sex. I whisper in blondie's ear, and she perks up quickly as she follows me to the bathroom. Quickly throwing each other into a stall, she begins undoing my belt and pants as I suck her lips into my mouth.

"My name is Isla," she breathlessly gets out.

"Great," I murmur into her mouth before she slides down my body, taking my pants and boxers down with her. It is when her hand grabs onto my bollocks as she glides my cock in her mouth. "Bloody hell," I whisper out as my head slams back on the wall of the stall, while my hands reach down to her head, helping her find her rhythm bobbing back and forth. I need to give her props, even through the gagging she has managed to take me all in. My tip slams the back of her throat over and over again. Her tongue twirls around my hardness and lips the tip before taking me all the way back in as she begins to suck harder. Speaking up, letting her know I am about to explode, she sucks harder while gripping my balls. My warmth slides down her throat as she swallows and sucks me dry. She pulls my pants up as she stands back to face me with the biggest smile on her face.

"Thank you, Isla," I say as I buckle my pants up. "May I return the favor?"

"O no," she says. "I have had my eye on you all night. Happy to assist, Mr. Stratton." I can only chuckle under my breath as we step out of the stall, because though most of the time many are not aware of who I am, I am always surprised by those that do. More surprised that it seems others prefer to use me before I can use them. She rinses her mouth out with aqua fresh she has in her bag, while I splash cold water on my face.

It is now three am, and I am being escorted out of the club by another fine blonde from one of the bachelorette parties to her car. Taking residence in the back seat, we strip each other down and shag. Shag in every position we can make happen in her sedan, while her bosom bounces in my face. G left an hour or so ago with the brunettes, leaving us betting who will not make it on to our transportation by departure. For me, five-fifty-five AM I am crawling into the motorcoach, barely making it to my bed before passing out face down.

Chapter 1: Fresh Market Saturday

This morning, Winston and I are up to spend some time around the fresh farmers market to grab a few items. Fresh honey is a must, along with some new jams from the Griffin family and maybe a fresh bouquet of flowers for the house. I decided to not even put Winston on leash once we got out of the car, as he loves to wander to each table and see who will pet him or give a special treat. Winston cracks me up as he is way more social than I am. He does not have a care in the world. I guess when you are a handsome fun loving teddy bear, you have the world at your paws. It is only ten in the morning on a Saturday, but this place is starting to get busy. The fresh farmers market takes place once a month, so us locals and nearby towns love to take full advantage of dropping in and stocking up. That is also why I get here early, to avoid the crowds.

Stopping to grab a few vegetables from the Henry farm table, I see Winston take off to three booths down the aisle. Knowing he won't go too far, I chat a little with Melissa and Melanie, the two teenage daughters of the Henry family. The girls let me know what books they are reading, their summer plans, if I have any book recs, *because I always do*, and I tell them I will put them aside for them to stop by this week to grab. After paying and thanking the girls, I place my items in my basket and walk in the direction I last saw Winston. Only soon to be almost taken out by my own dog, who comes flying between my legs and hides behind me.

"Oh, Winston, what did you do?"

"I will tell you what that damn dog of yours did!" an angry man yells back at me in a thick accent. I quickly look up at the man who is charging my way with his fist up in the air. Several eyes are on us now, as the man opens his mouth to speak again.

"That mutt of yours stole my breakfast biscuit. Does he have no manners?"

I only start to giggle because this man could not look any more out of place if he tried. He is dressed to the nines in what I can tell are designer jeans, shoes, and shirt. His hair is perfectly in place, and a body that is only accentuated by his form fitting clothes. I notice he does have a cast on his arm as it rests in a sling. He is dreamy to look at, and if his accent did not make his yelling seem somewhat endearing, I might have thought to punch him.

"Do you find this funny? Dog, like his owner, with no manners."

"Okay there, pal, take a breather. My apologies if my dog stole your biscuit. I am more than happy to give you money for a new one. Here take this." I reach out to hand him five dollars.

"I do not need your money. It is the principle that your dog has no manners and is not on a leash."

"Again, sir, my apologies. If you won't take my money, all I can do is apologize. He is a very friendly dog and most people around here know him, and if they don't, he soon makes friends with him. So I promise you, he met no harm, and judging by the look on his face and the fact that he is scared behind me, I am sure he feels awful about it."

"Bollocks! Just forget it," he huffs as he walks off, muttering to himself about how he got stuck in this small town.

I look over to Mrs. Baxter and the self proclaimed 'gossiping old lady group' and just shrug my shoulders. What else can I do at this point? Whistling for Winston to follow me, we head off to the car to load up and head home. All the while thinking to myself, what a pompous prick that guy was. I hope he does not plan on staying for the whole summer because he is not someone I want to have another encounter with.

Chapter 2: Concept of Time

Time is my enemy. Only when this life is over will it be my savior as it releases its digging and twisting clutch on me. It moves too fast in my few moments of life's enjoyment, but slow as a predator stalking his prey. Time is the predator as it is out to attack and torture my heart, my soul.

Last year after my accident, hospitalization and defeating loneliness, I was about to find a bit of enjoyment. Wandering the streets of London and the country landscapes as I was over there for an author convention. My best friend, Becca, happily tagged along, so we turned a four-day trip into eight. We wanted to take in as many sights we could since we were over the pond. The trip was not needed just for my own emotional and mental health, but for us to be able to reconnect. It was hard getting back stateside when taking separate connecting flights from New Jersey. Her to North Carolina, me back to Rhode Island. It felt like the days flew by, and now my days routinely drag on.

Bec has been my girl since pre-k. Growing up in a small island town, there was not much to do, other than going to the beach. Saying that, if there was a way to get in trouble, Bec would find it, and I was the one that had to talk us out of it or argue for a lesser punishment. We were and are still complete opposites, looks and personality. Bec is a tall, vivacious blonde with me standing five inches shorter and wavy black hair, with more curves to my hips then her. Barbie and Midge is what most of the town referred to us by. She moved away four years ago, following her husband Brian to North Carolina for a job promotion. They had my god-daughter Emma Kay, who I adore and hate not seeing her enough. To put it mildly, their daughter is very much Bec. A daredevil and jokester. Brian on the other hand is fairly straightlaced. Obeys the rulebook of life, a pharmacist because as much as he wanted to be a doctor, he passes out with the sight of blood. He treats Bec like a queen despite the hell she puts him through with her pranks, loud laughter in public, and the PDA she loves to give just to embarrass him. Every time she calls, there is a story of another shenanigan that has taken place. I am sure today is no different as I see her name pop up on my phone.

Answering the phone, I cheerfully yell, "Happy Mother's Day! What mischief did you and Emma cause today?"

"E! He is livid, and thanks!" Bec shrieks out amidst her laughing. "You know that balloon confetti TikTok trend?"

"Kinda."

"Okay so, Emma lured Brian into the kitchen by needing help getting a snack. I was hiding in the cabinets above the fridge, but before I rigged a balloon to drop on top of him and bust as he opened the door. There was no way this was going to work, right? Wrong! As soon as I heard him open that fridge door and balloon bust, I kicked open the cabinet door and shot off my confetti gun in his direction. There is confetti and glitter all over my kitchen and probably house as he stomped off. Here, sending you the video now." She is still laughing hysterically as I await the video. Ping! I open the notification and proceed to watch the video.

"Oh my gosh, Bec!" I exclaim, trying to hold in my laughter. "Is that glue?"

"Of course, girl. How else was everything going to stick." I can tell she is still rolling on the floor laughing. "I'll ask for forgiveness later in the bedroom. Besides, I had other reasons for calling you."

"Oh yeah? Other than to make sure I am alive." I try not to sound too annoyed, but she does call every day, even if just to make sure I answer the phone and am in a decent mood. I can't complain too much, she is my person, and I love her.

"So first, how are you? I know today is an awful reminder, though you mourn her daily."

"I am good, I promise. Just been keeping myself busy so as not to dwell on it. So, what else have you got for me?"

"Well okay, then… So Brian and I are planning our five-year anniversary trip for the fall. Thinking of Hawaii, Ireland, or the United Kingdom. No matter where we go, we want you to join us. We need another adventure."

"I am not imposing on your anniversary trip. But I am happy to stay behind to keep Emma."

"No, Brian's parents are coming with us to help with Emma. And I am not taking a no for an answer from you. I won't lie that England or Ireland are sounding great right now. We did not get to see it all, and I talked Brian's ear off with all the places and things we did do. WAIT! If we did England, Windsor would definitely be on the list, and we could hit up that pub again you loved so much. What was it called?"

"Oh, the Horse and Groom. I did love that place and its view of the castle. That whole town is a magical, serene place of history."

"Okay, this made my decision so much easier. I will start working out details. Check to see if there are any author, library or author conventions happening around the area also."

"You are too appeasing."

"That is what best friends are for. OOOOOH, do you think that pompous ass is still around?"

"Surely not. Ugh, why does God feel the need to create beautiful assholes? I still don't think I have ever been so turned on and insulted at once. It was bordering on disturbing how my mind and body were absorbing him." Bec is laughing loudly again because she knows how mortified I was. Not knowing what to do or say. I have never been approached in such a manner by a man thinking he was the devil himself and thought he needed to personally show me through Hell in such sexual acts. He looked like he made a deal with the devil with his perfect sinful looks and that devilish grin he gave, that made my insides want to turn inside out and touch him. His distinct, formal British husky-toned voice alluring me to listen and cave into his suggestions. Something about him let me know that no one told him no, and I was about to hear all about it. Until another handsome charming guy came up and whispered something in his ear. One more look at me as if trying to make a decision, and then he was gone. Both guys disappeared, and we never saw them again the rest of the trip. I do remember the bartender mentioning to another customer about those two being local, and some joke about them always in some rubbish either home or on their travels.

"Such beautiful memories traveling with you over there. We always have such grand adventures with the craziest stories to tell."

"We do, don't we? And more to come," I say as I hear Brian yelling Bec's name in the background. "Uh-oh, sounds like you are finally getting into trouble," I say, laughing.

"Nah, he will be fine. I will go strut myself into the bedroom, pull him into the shower while stripping his gooey glue-soaked clothes off. Then proceed to blow him after washing and massaging him clean. All will be right in the world in the next ten minutes."

"Bec…ewww… seriously, I do not need all the details, but go have fun."

Laughing, she mutters, "Bye love."

"Bye."

Honestly, if it wasn't for those two, I would truly believe love is dead. But alas, I just know love is not in the cards for me in any form.

"And the closer she was, the further apart she wanted to be. She just could not get it together, until she met him. - Hate is heavy."-Robert M. Drake Beautiful Chaos

Chapter 3: Storm is Rolling In

I am out for my morning run before the sun even rises. It is my favorite time to run out on the beach. Before it gets busy with all the beach-goers and teenagers wanting to lay out all day. All I hear are the waves rolling in with just enough light as the sun crests over the horizon. Feeling my phone vibrate, I pull my phone out of my pants pocket and see it is my sister calling. She calls every Monday like clockwork. We are not super close, but we are kind of all we have left as far as family goes. We text throughout the week as things come up, but I can always count on her phone calls on Monday.

"It is a bit early for you on a Monday, isn't it?" I ask when I answer.

"It is, but the little one is up, and Matt has to go into the office today for a board meeting, so figured I would check in before the day gets crazy since I ignored life yesterday."

"No, I totally get that, but it was your first Mother's Day, so I hope you enjoyed it some."

"I did. Matt and Charli made breakfast, and I had the day to do absolutely nothing, which was nice. But also, I felt I needed to sleep to not deal with the sorrow of Mom being gone."

"I bet. Well another one down, I guess."

"You holding up okay?"

"Yah, I am. Nothing new here, other than the out of towners seem to be rolling in early this season. I met some jackass Englishman yesterday. Like literally somewhere from around England. Even had the audacity to yell at Winston."

"Well, we know that is forbidden."

"Right! Though Winston did apparently steal his biscuit, but still. He caused a whole scene even after I offered to buy him a new one. I am telling you, Kat, he looked like he walked straight out of a GQ magazine or something. I usually hear about all the incoming celebrities or newbies, but I have no idea who this guy was. Anyways, that is about all the excitement for me at the moment. You?”

“Not much here either. Matt has some traveling to do this month, so planning on joining him on a few adventures, and Charli and I can go sight-seeing.”

“That will be fun and good for you all. O, let me go get Winston, he is chasing the crabs again. Apparently he is not remembering the pain of being pinched.”

Laughing, she says, “Okay, well I will check in later.”

“Okay, bye.”

I start my run again, letting out a whistle for Winston to follow. Luckily he does because I can see those little crab eyes sticking out of their sand holes just waiting to attack. Running slowly backward, as I watch for Winston to catch back up with me.

UMPH!

What the hell? I groan as I turn over on the ground to see what I just ran into.

“Watch where you are going!” *Shit, I know that damn voice.*

“Maybe you need to watch where you are going.” He quickly looks down at me with regret.

“Here, let me help you up.” He gives me his hand and pops me up like I am a kernel of popcorn.

“Thanks, but really, you should pay attention out here. Not just because others are running, but there are other living creatures out here too.”

“Point taken.” He keeps staring at me very intently like he wants to say something else. Then he looks down to see a sand covered Winston, panting next to me. “It is you from yesterday. Is this really how my day is going to go?”

All I can do is look at him in astonishment and decide not to give the time of day anymore. Moving around him, I begin to jog when I hear him holler out to me, “Where are you going, beautiful bird?”

Without evening turning around, I flip my hand around and show him my kind of bird. Only a pompous ass thinks he can insult and compliment you in one breath.

After a busy day at the library, I decide to go ahead and stop by the store to grab a few things for the week since the upcoming weather is not going to be pleasant. As it seems, most of the locals had the same idea. Meaning the weather channel must have upped the severity of the impending strong winds, whipping rain, and possible storm surge. As we all push our carts down the aisles trying to find whatever we need, I pull up the weather app on my phone while grazing down the deli and produce aisles to get sandwich meat, cheese, and pineapple.

"No dog with you?" I hear behind me. *Seriously, who the hell did I piss off today?* Taking a deep breath, I turn around to be faced with the Englishman for the second time today.

"Are you stalking me or something? How do you keep finding me?"

"I was about to ask you the same question. Luckily for me, I can now identify you by that divine arse of yours."

"Excuse me?" I spit out, trying to cough back my anger. This man infuriates me with his damn good looks and thinks he is God's gift to the world. "Please stop staring at my ass and leave me out of your sights completely."

"Not sorry. You literally made me stare at it this morning when you ran away from me."

"Um, okay. I…I am just going to go."

"No, wait. Please?" he begs as he gently grabs my upper arm.

"Oh, good to know you have some manners yourself. But can you take your hand off of me?" I ask sternly.

Pulling away, he looks at me like he did this morning. Regret, lust, want, and angst all rolled into his glistening forest green eyes.

"Have we met before? I mean other than this weekend, have I met you?"

"Seriously doubt it. Lived here my whole life, and I don't associate myself with pompous pricks," I say and turn around to leave. Luckily, he does not follow or so I thought.

"Can I help you with that?" he asks as he comes up behind me in the checkout line.

"No, thank you. I believe my two hands got this compared to your one working one." I wince, feeling extremely guilty as the words leave my mouth.

"Damn, you are harsh. Beautiful, but harsh."

"Gosh, I am so sorry. I really didn't mean it. Just already in a mood, and you are just infuriating me today."

"Happy to know I am making at least some impression on you," he says with a smolder.
Rolling my eyes in return, I quickly pay and grab my bagged items.

"Have a nice day," I yell over my shoulder and leave. Only to call Bec and fill her in on my day. I know she will get a kick on this newcomer.

Chapter 4: When Life Gives Us Lemons

It is two AM in the morning, as I am staring out the large bay window that overlooks the water's edge with a view of the lighthouse. I let out a sigh of angst as the lighthouse sends out its identification light, highlighting the white caps of the surging waves. Indicating a storm is rolling in; it will be the first storm of the summer. I used to love this quiet time in the early hours, when a storm was breaking way onto the island, but now it brings a chill down my spine, an ache in my left leg, along with high anxiety of something going array.

As for the last four years, a storm has only brought back memories, heartache and life going amiss. Lost in one's own thoughts, I suddenly feel a big wet nose pushing up against my arm. "O, hey there boy. Did I wake you?" I ask as I scratch his big brown head. He jumps up on the window seat next to me, laying down with his head on my upper thigh. "You are such a good boy, Winston. You won't ever leave me, huh?" Winston then covers my hand with his paw as he lets out a large sigh himself, falling back to sleep.

Taking a sip of my hot English tea with honey, I turn to look back out the window, trying to grasp at any perspective on my own life. Never thought that at the age of thirty, I would have come completely parentless, single, and just trying to move through life unaffected. Ex-fiance left over a year ago and never returned, decided to stay in Boston. It has been three years this December since Mama left this earth and fifteen months since my own dad decided to just disappear off the face of the same planet. Pushing through another Mother's Day with such heavy loss has me defeated. Feeling alone is an understatement.

As much as I would love to ignore all the despairing parts of my life, I know it is nearly impossible in this small town off the coast of Rhode Island. Watch Hill, with a population of one hundred and fifty-four and counting; at least for the summer anyway. I'm the island's only librarian, which also means the island's social event planner. Growing up on this island, living in the house my parents left me, when Mama passed, working at the same library I grew up spending most of my childhood days. I know everyone's gossip as well as everyone knowing about my own boring life.

Along with no one approving of the long-term boyfriend, now ex-finance as of a year ago, Connor. We had met back at Boston college, becoming friends first, then after graduation, he persuaded me to date him. I liked his easy-going personality and sense of security he gave me. Though he was a Boston native, and I wanted to head back home, he always made it a point through the first several years to make time for us and surprise me with trips. We were happy, and I knew back then that he loved me. But the last few years, he had become more of a workaholic, traveling more for his family's accountant firm, almost as if not wanting to be around. I already confronted him on cheating six months before we ended, but he told me that was the last thing he would do. That he just did not know how to handle the mood swings I always had, and thought it was safer to be gone, then be on the other end of my striking wrath. For it all to end with him not coming back at all. Not going to lie, I was taken back. Realizing that I truly had not been myself in years since losing my mama. That the whole situation seemed to have siphoned my soul away.

Walking into the library this morning, I began taking the necessary precautions of boarding up the stained glass windows on the northeast side of the library to protect them. The full brunt of the storm is just several hours away. Afterwards, I go about brewing coffee and tea at the drink station, then organizing yesterday's returns. The same routine I have had for years now. Not even the locals who stop in to gossip about the morning news can throw me off. I always listen and answer politely while moving about the library as they follow me around. Young and old alike. This morning is no different.

"Good morning, Miss Emelia," little Oliver says as he runs into the library and over to me.

"Good morning, Oliver. Isn't it a little early for you to be up causing chaos on your first summer morning?"

"You are funny, Miss Emelia. It is but, but my parents had to run to Mr. Jacobs' this morning to grab more lumber to help old lady Annette with her fence before it blows away with the storm, plus my mom wanted me to drop off some fresh lemons."

He continues to ramble on as I nod my head acknowledging all his stories. The bells ring on the front door again, causing Oliver and myself to poke our heads out the side of the bookshelf. "How are you today, Mrs. Baxter?" I ask.

"I am fine, dear, just came by to check on the arrangements for the Summer Bash for the weekend."

"All good to go, Mrs. Baxter. The storm should pass by Thursday afternoon, so that gives us time to clean up any damage then set up for Friday night."

"You truly are the best my dear! If only your mother could see how you are turning out…"

"Oh, Gina Baxter, do not make that girl cry this morning. You know her mother smiles down on her every day," widowed Mrs. Galant states as she interrupts Mrs. Baxter.

Giggling at the two old ladies bickering, I thank both of them for being so kind and for thinking of Mama.

"Now, Mrs. Galant, what can I help you with this morning? I already let Mrs. Baxter know that all is a go with the Summer Bash for Friday."

"Perfect! But actually, I came to ask a favor…" I see her begging pleading smile make an appearance. "You know how sometimes you rent out your guest room for those in need?"

Hesitantly and wide-eyed, I say, "For certain occasions and depending on who it is. Why? Who do you have in mind? As I thought everyone accounted for coming in was either staying at the Ocean Villa or has rented an Airbnb?"

"Well, we have someone already here, but a few pipes busted in their Airbnb early this morning, and he needs a place to stay while the mess is cleaned up and fixed. It could take at least a week. I have already tried the Ocean Villa which is already booked up and The Irving's place. They are not leaving for Europe until the end of the month. You are really my last hope, Emelia."

"Who is this person? Other than a complete stranger; needless to say, a man you want to stay with me?"

"He is Lucas Stratton, the race car driver." Mrs. Galant says cheerfully, then pauses for a reaction.

"This is so cool! Finally, someone other than a movie star coming into town. This guy is known as "The Playboy" of racing, always winning, drives with class, but has a hot temper and will wreck people. Dad says he is too good for his own good. Whatever that is supposed to mean, but I did read an article he likes to party and have a good time. Like who does not like to party? Most people hate his style, but I think he is awesome. Miss Emelia, he races in the British GT series, but recently signed to the American series under the Privé team driving. He drives a McLaren! This is really the coolest thing ever to happen here!" Oliver exclaims.

"I honestly have no clue who either of you are talking about. Yet still amazed how much racing knowledge you have, kid… Mrs. Galant, I am not sure about him staying with me."

"I am begging you, Emelia. He really is looking for a place to get away from it all per his agent, and he is still recovering from surgery. I had to beg his agent to calm him down and keep him here. You know we count on summer tourism, so the last thing we need is a horrible review for our quaint small town. If I had somewhere else to place him, I would, but your house is beautiful with a stunning view. Plus, guests never want to leave, stating you are such a great hostess."

"Fine, but only until next Friday. He will have to go somewhere else if his place is not ready. Does he need to shift houses now, or can he come by later?"

"Now would be good, so he can get settled…" Mrs. Galant says scaredly.

"Ugh, of course…um…the extra key is in the daisy flower pot next to the turtle. You can go ahead and let him in and help get him settled. I will run over there at about one o'clock to check on him."

Shaking my hand, Mrs. Galant thanks me and quickly turns to leave before I have the chance to ask any more questions and change my mind. Watching her out the window, I see her whispering to herself and giggling as she gets into her car.

For the rest of the morning, Oliver brings me up to speed about the GT series, along with differences between the American and British series and all Lucas Stratton racing stats. Well at least he has one little fan in this town. Oliver's dad, Jake, owns his own restoration car garage and races on the weekends as a hobby. Jake has become a small-town celebrity in his own right and that is about the extent I know of it. Needless to say, Oliver is obsessed with all thing's car related, and at ten years old, he has already rebuilt his own go-kart engine and helps his dad at work and on the track. Before I know it, it is one o'clock, and I realize I need to head home to check on the *guest.* After putting the sign up to return an hour, I jump on the bike and head down the pathway home. Getting closer to the driveway, I spot a shiny, fancy red car sitting there. Great, so much for him wanting to lie low while he is here. That car screams, LOOK AT ME. Walking into the house, I make my way to the kitchen, only to find it in a colossal mess.

"What in the world happened here?" I speak out loud as I start picking up empty wrappers and left out sandwich meat, throwing it all in the trash.

"I am sorry, Miss, I have not had a chance to come back in here to clean up."

Startled, I look over in shock. "Who are you? You look a little older than to be this famous race car driver I keep hearing about. No offense."

"Yes, excuse me, Miss, I am Lucas Stratton's agent, Kent Lawson. I just got back from picking up his groceries and necessities. It seems he helped himself to some lunch while I was out. I will replace whatever he used."

"It's fine. Not that big of a deal." All the while thinking to myself, I did not sign up to be this man's maid or babysitter. "Are you supposed to be staying here as well, Mr. Lawson?"

"No, and please call me Kent. I just flew in with him to get him settled, and then the whole pipe fiasco happened this morning, so I had to delay my flight. We really appreciate you letting him stay here. He currently has his wrist in a cast and arm in a sling post-surgery but prefers to do everything himself. So don't feel the need to tend to him. It was also best to remove him from the public eye, sooner than later. If you have any problems with him, here is my card if you need me."

Looking dumbfounded, I ask, "Public scene? Post-Surgery?" as agent Kent realizes he said too much.

"Well, I must be off to catch my flight. Best of luck and remember to call me if you need anything. I have also already deposited the money in your account for rent and things. Bye."

As he quickly runs out the door, leaving me in a state of shock, Winston comes padding in. "Where were you through all the chaos? Probably begging for some food from a stranger, huh?" I ask, rubbing his ears. I then pull my phone out of my pocket, searching for Lucas Stratton. Scrolling through the headlines, I cannot believe who is in my house. Lucas, racecar driver Caught for Racing on Public Road, Badboy Lucas, Breaks Another Heart, Rumor Has It, Lucas Stratton Needing an Intervention, LS Signing to the America GT Series with Prive, Stratton Replacing Dougel in the McClaren in the American GT Series, Injured Stratton

using the Next Month off to Heal and Rest, and the newsfeed
just keeps going. Trust me, his looks were not lost on me
either. A look alike to Adam Demos, but not sure if he can
even hold a candle to the looks of this dirty blonde god of a
man. A quick thought passes through my mind that he looks
familiar. *No damn way…* It is that pompous Englishman.
Again, who did I piss off to be thrown into such a fate?
Snapping out of it to focus on what I am getting myself into,
trying to get my thoughts together and pray he is not a
nightmare to live with.
Sharing my own explicit thoughts with an attentive Winston,
I lay out the ground rules that will need to be enforced while
the pretty, party boy is here. Guessing I will approach him
when he decides to come out, I decide to head back to the
library for the remainder of the day.
"Bye, Winston, be a good boy!"

Lucas's POV

Not knowing someone is lurking behind the corner
listening to her out loud thoughts, I step out into the open.
Winston walks over to me for some ear rubbing, and I take
another look around the house. He has finally warmed up to
me after I groveled and apologized by laying on the floor
with him, giving him belly rubs. I already did some snooping
earlier when Kent brought me here and dropped me off to run
some errands. It seems I am living with an intellectual
bookworm according to the wall of built-in bookshelves in
the living room that is filled to the edges. Then on the other
wall, there is a stone fireplace, with shiplap above that the
TV is hanging on, but also surrounded by more built-in
bookshelves on either side filled with mostly books and a few
pictures with just a small plush couch facing its direction.
The back of the living room has a large bay window that
overlooks the ocean, where I can already imagine her sitting

at the window seat when I spot an unfolded blanket and a book on it. Picking the book up, *Sold on a Monday,* I grimace. Well that looks and even sounds depressing, I think to myself as I toss it back on to the window seat. The rest of the room opens to the kitchen with a door that leads to the outside deck in between the two rooms. I see the door to her bedroom near the wall of bookshelves, but I do like to think of myself as a gentleman and not invade her complete privacy as I glance once more at a few pictures on the shelves.

Turning back to a tail wagging Winston, I murmur, "I assume your mom does not think too highly of me, huh, guy? She is more beautiful than I recall from yesterday." Winston turns in a circle and barks, almost as a warning. "Okay, *okay,* I won't do anything stupid. How about we get some fresh air and go for a walk?" With that, Winston runs off to grab his leash for me. Once linked, we both head out to walk the town. I mutter to myself, "Time to rely on the Stratton charm." Knowing I have to apologize for being an incorrigible arse.

Winston makes a point to stop at all the places on the strand that he knows gives out treats and has the water bowls out to enjoy. I personally don't seem to mind too much, as everyone knows it is Emelia's dog, so it is helping me find out a little more about her with each visit. I am also enjoying the fact that even though quite a few people are familiar with me in this town, there are no paparazzi. It is nice to be able to have actual real conversations with other people. Instead of the usual posse or girls just wanting to hang for my own ego or themselves. I can be whoever I want to be here, but also have been warned about being on my best behavior. Letting Winston lead the way, we both soon find ourselves in front of the library. Before I can even reach to open the door, the door opens as a customer walks out, and Winston quickly takes off, pulling the leash out of my good hand, sending me down to my knees, holding the door open with my body.

I hear yelling, pulling my head in the direction of her voice. "Winston! What are you doing here? Please tell me you did not escape again?" Emelia asks, walking around the check-out counter. Barking, he runs back to the door, Emelia following behind him. She finds me embarrassingly trying to get back up, with one able arm to pull myself up with and dusting off my jeans.

"Oh my gosh, Are you okay? Oh my god, your arm!" I shake my head in disbelief of what just happened and not to show my bruised ego.

"No, I am fine. Just didn't expect him to take off like that." I look up from the ground to her. *Shit, she is the most beautiful bird I have ever seen with her flawless serene features and haunting eyes.*

"Yah, he gets excited when he sees me, hates for me to leave him alone at home."

"I can sympathize with him." A grin sweeps across my face, leaving Emelia's cheeks flushed in red. When my eyes meet hers, it's like fireworks going off around us.

"Um, anyways… Why are you guys here? Are you sure we do not need to get your wrist and shoulder checked out?" she asks, concern lacing her tone.

"It seemed he was up for showing me around town. I'm also not a fan of staying cooped up for a long period of time. I promise you, it is fine." *Not really fine, my whole arm is throbbing like bloody hell, but I am not telling her that.*

"Gotcha. Well Winston has a way of getting his way, so don't let him fool you otherwise." Emelia lets out a sigh that I deem as a loving but agitated one, as she rubs Winston's ears, making my heart skip with such a pleasing sound. She is beautiful with her wavy black as midnight hair blowing in the breeze, causing me to catch her scent. Something between vanilla, honey, and paper. I may need to get closer to really decipher, but either way, it's inviting.

Laughing, I say, "I will keep that in mind. But I think we had a great time, right, buddy?" As I lean over to scratch his back.

"He seems to be taken to you, which means you might be more of a decent person than I thought … Oh my gosh, did I say that last part out loud?" Wide eyed and blushing in shame, she utters, "I am so so so sorry. I am not out to insult you. I don't even know you outside of your stellar first impressions."

"Honestly, it is a breath of fresh air, so no harm done. Just sounds like I need to convince you of what kind of person I really am outside the news and the last few days." As I just stare at her, I get completely lost in those amber colored eyes.

"I guess so…. But for now, I do probably need to get back in there, so I can finish a few things before closing up for the day. I can keep Winston here with me, if you want to continue touring the town."

"I am actually enjoying this view right now. Anything I can help with?" I can tell she is completely flushed and taken back when she answers.

"Sure, I still have to finish boarding up some windows before the storm blows in tomorrow."

"Lead the way," I murmur as I place my hand on the small of her back. Winston happily pads behind us. I do notice as I watch her intently at times, she has a slight limp to her left side. It is practically unnoticeable if you weren't looking for it. For me, I feel the need to study every inch of her.

Two hours later, after Emelia finished her library tasks and I helped put boards up over the windows, the two of us, plus Winston, set off down the street back to the house. By this time, the sky has turned a dark grayish purple, as the clouds are swirling above us, causing trees and plants to sway rapidly, along with the water line rising quickly on to shore. The three of us make it into the house right when the bottom of the sky opens up, pouring heavy droplets to the ground.

"That was close!" Emelia says, laughing. Even her laugh catches me off guard and turns my insides on fire.

I laugh right along with her. "Are all summer storms this fierce?" I ask, while grabbing a towel from her hand to run roughly through my wet strands of hair, as they seamlessly fall back into place. Being from the UK, I am used to the drizzle and downpours, but not typically when it is sunny one minute then cloudy the next or being accompanied by strong wind gusts.

I catch Emelia in a memorized stare in my direction. "Are you checking me out?"

Her amber eyes quickly dart away. "Um, NOPE… just running through a checklist in my head. Besides, you are coming on pretty strong with a complete stranger you just met recently, aren't you?" she says as she walks down the hallway and apparently does not even bother to wait for my response as she continues to talk. "Really just depends on the year, the season, the tides, and the mood of mother nature. I have to say this might be the worst one we have had in the last five years. I can tell by the aching chill my body has, as the storm moves closer in." She pauses, stopping herself from continuing. "We honestly never know what it will bring until it's gone. Welcome to Watch Hill."

A kiss may ruin a human life -
Oscar Wilde

Chapter 5: Try to Make Lemonade

Lucas has not left my side since we got back to the house. He even tried to help make dinner, which ended up a disaster, with chopped vegetables in disarray, making my kitchen look like a "Veggie Tale" crime scene. Tossing him the lemons I received from Oliver's mom this morning, I ask, "Care to make some lemonade?" As I pull out the hand pressed juicer, he looks at the juicer, then the lemons and back to me. Smirking, I murmur, "Let me show you." I slice the lemons in half, then grab one to place on top of the press, then press down as hard as I can, causing me to stand on my tiptoes to get some extra strength to push down.

Now his six-two self is laughing at me. "Aren't you petite and cute."

I begin to walk away, but he mildly grabs my elbow, pulling me in front of him at the counter. He precedes placing a lemon on the press, and carefully wrapping his large hand on top of mine, we push the lemon into the presser together. Such a simple act has turned sensual and heated. Instead of letting me get back to cooking dinner, he keeps me there repeating the steps, every so often leaning down into the nape of my neck breathing just so lightly it tickles. After we juice all eight lemons, he releases me like I was never there and goes about finishing it, adding some water and a few sliced strawberries. Shaking my head, I head back over to the stove to pull the chicken ranch casserole out. Placing it on the table along with the salad and sadly chopped sauteed vegetables, we eat and have light conversation about the day and weather.

This evening has felt natural and easy going. At this moment, I am not feeling completely alone. I know it won't last, but for now, I can at least try to enjoy myself and step a little out of my comfort zone. My phone rings so I answer it and walk into my bedroom, shutting the door.

"Help me, Bec. There is a sex God in my house right now." She begins laughing.

"Please tell me you plan on taking full advantage of him, E."

"Have you forgotten who your best friend is? Not a tramp. Besides, he is such bad news and makes me feel a certain way. Did you not look at the news articles I sent you?"

"I did, and let's get this straight. He is the tramp, not you. Therefore, you can take full advantage of him without feeling guilty or floozie."

"I am so glad this makes you so delighted, and you find my own discomfort amusing, Bec."

"The stars are aligning for you, E, take advantage. Take this gift and abuse the hell out of it."

"Oh wow, did some more background digging, he is from Berkshire. You should ask him about that pub you love so much and pry him for cool places to stay and see when we go."

"Sure, let me ask him for recs after I ask him to screw me."

"That's the spirit," she cheers on. "I have to get Emma to bed, or she will be a diabolical witch."

"Jesus, Bec…. not my sweet Emma."

"Shit, it has been six months since you've seen her and a week since you have facetimed with her. I am sleeping with one eye open right now, as she is sneaking out of her bed at night or early in the morning. She hides under our bed and grabs whoever's legs try to roll out of bed first. Don't even dare to try and look beforehand, because she probably has some hideous mask that Brian's mom keeps buying her. And the terrible two tantrums are just as bad as everyone says."

"I am not laughing at you but with you. Hang in there, and you three will be out here in a month-ish and have her all to myself for a bit. Plus, we have a lot of kid activities at the library this summer."

"You are my favorite friend for a reason. Ohh, she is running around the house naked. Gotta go, bye." I hang up, laughing and shaking my head in astonishment. Like I said, Emma Kay is all Becca.

I walk out of my bedroom and see him still sitting at the kitchen table scrolling through his phone.

"Hey, the rain has stopped for now, so I am going to sit out back for a bit, feel free to join me if you want."

He nods as I slide the door open and embrace the post rain smell mixed with the ocean breeze before stepping out and closing the door behind me. Leaning back in my chair, I close my eyes, taking in the roar of the ocean, the sounds of seagulls bickering and the calmness that comes over me. Nothing like the smell of the ocean mixed in with the rain that just poured. Bringing me back to the time of my childhood where I thought my family was happy. Where my dad would take my sister and I out fishing after a good rain. Said it was the best time to catch a "big one." My mama would watch from this very spot, smiling and laughing as I lost my Snoopy fishing rod to something large and unknown, and my sister's My Little Pony rod broke in half. Dad was trying to get us to be able to hold on to the large deep sea fishing rod he had that was heavy, and I swear at the time, the reel and spool was larger than my head. He always managed to catch sharks on it. But always let us release them. Maybe that time was real, and we were content. That was before Mama got sick and Dad started the unthinkable affair. Hmph. How weird it is looking back on life with a different perspective. Wishing I still had on rose colored glasses.

I hear the door slide open but keep looking out into the darkness. Lucas pulls a chair over next to me and props his feet up on the end table.

"Wow, you really do have a great view out here. I can't wait to really take it in during the day. This must be your spot."

"What makes you say that?" I ask.

"Well, it is the most relaxed I have seen you all day. And being that I just met you, I can tell you are somewhat introverted with yourself. As you seem to care and love those around you. Everyone in town adores you but worries about you."

"HA. Worries about me, huh? Please enlighten me on what they all told you."

"Actually, they said it was your story to tell, just that you have been emotionally hurt over and over again and some mention of an accident."

"That is too much of a heavy topic to share with someone I just met. But long story short, my mama passed away in a heart wrenching way. Most of the time I feel like she left me way too soon, but I had to respect her wishes. I have an ex-fiancé, and I could probably tell you where my dad is, but not hundred percent sure." Taking a pause for a sip of tea, then looking up at Lucas to be met with his inquisitive gaze. "One day I will face it head on, but for now, I will just try to live my life the way she would have wanted me to and ignore the rest."

"Seems like you miss her a lot…sorry for making you all melancholy. Was not my intention."

I reach to place my hand on his arm, getting lost in his dark green eyes that remind me of walking through an evergreen forest at dusk. "It's fine, really." Lucas must have sensed I was about to pull back, so he swiftly but gently placed his hand on top of mine. Smiles pass between us before settling back in our chairs. My mind runs through all the things I don't deal with, Becca's words about using him and how I got to this point. Thinking I should go to bed, as tomorrow brings a long day of waiting out the storm. Sitting up quickly, I must have spooked Lucas as he turns and stands as soon as I do. Our bodies collide. I can feel the heat radiating off of him. His hand lifts and slowly pushes the strand of hair out of my face by tucking it behind my ear.

"Look, I need to apologize for my behavior over the last couple of days. I was utterly an arse, but it is my shield from people getting too close. Especially when I am in a foreign place. So I am sorry."

"Thank you for that, and apology accepted. Just try to be yourself if there is a kinder you wrapped up in all of that. The town will be more accepting as well."

"Thank you, and yes, there is. … I know I just met you, but I have this desire to make those sorrowful eyes of yours' glister."

"Wow, you move quick! But please don't. I am not another girl that needs your tacky overused pickup lines."

"Emelia," he murmurs my name reverently as he bends down to kiss me on the cheek, then pausing before moving to my lips. It is soft and gentle, but possessive. Making it feel like electric sparks are pinging between us. As I am about to push him off, he speaks up, "I deserve that, especially if you investigated me and how I have acted. But that was not a pickup line. Good night, Emelia." He walks back into the house, rendering me speechless.

Chapter 6: For the Love of a Small Town

I rushed out of the house on my bike as soon as I could this morning and have been at the library for three hours already, not able to bring myself to do much of anything. Slowly putting books up and going through boxes of new orders. My mind, wandering back to that kiss. To those soft lush lips that tasted like a smooth bourbon.

Mrs. Galant pulls me out of my thoughts. "Emelia dear, how was last evening? The two of you faring okay?"

"Yes, Mrs. Galant. All is fine." Trying to deter her from talking about him, I smoothly change the subject. "I already have a team of highschoolers lined up to clean up the beach tomorrow evening, so we can start setting up for the Summer Bash. Please let Mrs. Baxter know all is covered when you see her at Bingo later. I am about to head out for the day. Marcy is coming in to cover the afternoon, until the storm hits."

"Okay, dear. Is our handsome race car driver doing well and fitting in?"

"Being it has not been quite twenty-four hours yet; I would say he is fine. But feel free to stop by and check up on him or take him off my hands any time."

"Oh, my. Looks like he was already under your skin at the market the other day, just give it time." she states giggling.

Now trying to hide my own intentions, I say, "What- No, just not used to sharing space with someone."

"Well, I am sure you two will be just dandy. Just give it time, my dear, give it time."

"You do remember he is supposed to be going back to his rental or somewhere else at the end of next week. That was the deal."

"Of course, of course. Just saying enjoy your time together. Oh, and bring him tomorrow to help set up. I know he has one arm in a sling, but that doesn't mean we can't put the other one to work… See you later, dear."

She is gone before I can refute her. I sure hope she is not trying to play matchmaker with the hot playboy and the librarian. I ride my bike to the store to grab some items for dinner and more deli meat for sandwiches. Only to be stopped by everyone asking how Lucas is doing and if we have hit it off yet. I am not sure mortified is a strong enough word for how I feel about all this talk in a matter of twenty-four hours. This is definitely not the first time my name has been on the town's lips. I have graced it with my mom passing, my dad's long-time affair, my dad leaving, Connor leaving me, and much more in between.

Once home and in the kitchen unloading groceries, I realize I have not been greeted by Winston. I start calling his name, nothing. So, I start to subtly panic as I make my way to my bedroom, down the hall, opening every door, until I get to *his*. I knock lightly, just to check, but then open it. The man is sound asleep in just his Calvin Klein boxers on top of the covers, with my traitor of a dog snoring right next to him. I quietly tip toe over to get Winston, who I must calm him down when he realizes I am home before exiting his room. Last minute, I grab a blanket and gently drape it over Lucas and then leave.

"What good of a guard dog are you, Winston?" I ask, as he paws at my leg. Patting his head, we curl up on the couch while I read a book. A few hours later, Playboy emerges from his room in at least shorts and tee this time. He still looks sexy as his hair is all ruffled, looking relaxed. *Focus.*

"We probably have about two hours or so before we lose power, so if you want to take a shower, now is the time." I start pulling out USB chargers from the side drawer in the kitchen. "These are charged and ready if you need to plug your phone or any electronics in. I am going to run to the mudroom to grab some extra candles and flashlights. Oh, and with no air tonight, your bedroom will get pretty muggy and hot, so you are more than welcome to join Winston and I out here in the living room," I state as he gazes back at me for some sense of reaction. He is staring wide-eyed at me like I am crazy. "I am so sorry, Lucas, for all the craziness and running around. I know this is least from what you expected coming here, let alone my hospitality manners have not been the greatest. You must be ready to leave and head home as soon as you can at this point," I continue as I am turning circles in the kitchen, opening cabinets and drawers, while gathering emergency items. Ever since my accident, storms make my skin itch, my body ache, and just overall antsy.

Usually, it is just me and Winston, now I have another person to worry about.

"Emelia, calm down." Placing his hands on both my shoulders, he holds me in place. Having to look down at my barely five-four stature, he says, "You have no reason to apologize. I am fine, and this situation is fine. It seems I lucked out being in great company with the two of you." I politely smile back then continue to panic on the inside as I try to calmly finish gathering everything.

Several hours into the night, we remain awake, sharing both ends of the window seat, listening to the storm wreaking havoc around us. Lightning flashing through the sky every few seconds, allowing us to catch a peak at the surging white capped waves charging everything in their path. The lighthouse casting the storm warning beacon into the darkness. As now all power is out on the island, so the room is only lit by candlelight.

"So, can I ask what you are thinking about? As you seem to suddenly have a smirk on your face." I ask.

"Oh, nothing really. It has been a long time since I sat with someone and just relaxed and had a real conversation. Have someone listen without wanting something in return or trying to relate."

Nodding in agreement, I take a sip of tea.

"Have to say the company has been really nice too… So, tell me more about you. It must have been awesome growing up in this small sea town."

"It has its own pros and cons, as I am sure everywhere does. But I would not trade it for anything. This town is not only my home, but my family. Several are not the easiest to get along with, but without them, I would not have survived the last few years. This town can for sure humble you if you let it."

Stopping myself from saying much more as I catch a glimpse of his stunning side profile as the candlelight flickers around us. It has been an afternoon and night of strong sexual tension and connection. But he has been nothing but a gentleman helping me get things ready for the storm and inquiring about me. Though a big part of me thinks this must be how he catches his prey. How he lures them in with his alluring sexiness, accent, and possibly genuine politeness, to then sleep with them and then break their hearts. Though I am also sure he is not lacking the breed of female that have no problem using him for a one-night stand to tick another off their celebrity hook-up list.

Nodding his head in acknowledgement, he lifts his eyes slightly in my direction. "I'll keep that in mind… So rough past? Care to share anymore?"

Looking back out the window, sipping my tea again, I murmur, "Not particularly at the moment."
He oddly rubs my arm, like telling me it's all going to be okay. After a few lingering moments, we both smile, relaxing back into our nooks within the window seat. My body is already feeling heated and flushed. Internally telling myself to back down, it's just been a hot minute since you've been close to a man, it could be a hot spoon touching you for all you know!
"So, what made you become a librarian?" he asks.
"Meaning of all the jobs and cool things to do in the world, why would I choose to be in a building surrounded by boring books all day?" I throw back, and he laughs.
"Not what I was thinking, but since you went that route, do tell."

"I have loved reading since I could read. Always had to have a story read to me at night before I could read, and as soon as I could, I would sneak under my sheets with a flashlight and read until I fell asleep. I am pretty sure my mama knew, but never said anything to me about it. But yah, I have always just found comfort in reading. My life was not a lot of thrills, and as I got older, it became my escape from the real-world shit that was going on around me. I also love being able to read about new far-off places to add to my bucket list, or biographies of interesting people. I am quite fond of history, learning the how's and why's of time. Of course, though, my favorite is romance."

"Really?" he asks half-jokingly. "I would have taken you for more of a serial killer and murder mystery girl."

"Far from it. Nothing about dying or reading about someone being murdered excites me. If it so happens to be part of the plot I am reading, then fine, but you will not see me reading an entire novel about it. I guess part of me still wants to believe in the romantic notion of love or at least read about other people being so fortunate whether it is real or not." He nods his head in understanding. "My mama and I used to share a love for reading also. She did not read a whole lot while raising my sister and I, but every now and then she would dabble, but really started reading books with all her downtime at dialysis. Then you had my dad who loved to read about the World Worlds and Pearl Harbor. I guess you could say my reading also stems from him, especially my love for history.

"Books are so much more than just paper between the bindings. They are someone's life explained, someone's imagination coming to life for them on paper, a person's love story or grievance that could be another person's saving grace. And there is no better feeling for me in my job, then being able to recommend a book to someone and they come back to tell me how much they loved it, that they related to it, they do not feel so alone or even helped them make a decision. I feel like I am doing my small part in the world by helping others, well at least in this town anyways. If you are ever participating in book trivia, I am your girl. The number of books I have read, quotes I have memorized, and books I know plots by heart, is slightly maddening at times. So yah, there is your warning on that.”

Lucas lets out this sexy laugh and sigh that has my thighs squeezing together with another urge as Bec’s words stream through my thoughts. *You have been given a gift, abuse the hell out of it.*

“You are a very intriguing person, Emelia, and I am totally taking you up on that trivia game. I can relate. Racing is not an escape for me, but like my life depends on it. If I am not able to push the limits behind a car a few times a month, I honestly think I would completely have lost the plot. Even in the most precarious of situations, risks must be taken. No risks, no rewards, and that is part of why I love it so much. I think of nothing else once my helmet goes on. Nothing else matters in the world, but that one goal. The goal to win. The moment where you are going as fast as you can, when all instincts kick in like you are on the edge of a cliff to survive, but you and the car become one, giving the best type of buzz. You feel electric, you feel alive with every corner and lap behind you, as you begin to approach the finish line. The feeling of knowing you are the one crossing the finish line first is like no other, and what you dream of as a racecar driver.

“Wow, that sounds really intense. Dangerous, but intense. Not sure I could ever do something as wild as that.”

“I would like to take you for a ride sometime. My McClaren race car is a one-seater, but my current McLaren sitting in your driveway can be just as fun on a back road when you are up for it.”

“Ummm, I’ll keep that in mind. Maybe in an emergency I will take you up on the offer.”
He lets out that damn sexy laugh again, but luckily saved by Winston, who has placed his head on the window seat, making soft growling sounds, hinting it’s way past his own

bedtime. Laughing, I state I better go lay down and cuddle with the grumpy bear, so he behaves tomorrow.

"He really does run this place, huh?" Lucas states, laughing.

"The whole town to be exact. But he deserves all the love attention," I say while I squish his face in and rubbing it in. Winston lets out a bark in an agreement.

"I can see that. Well, you two get some rest, I will probably be awake a little longer."

"Okay, well good night, then.," I murmur as I lay down to cuddle with Winston in my arms.

<u>Lucas's POV</u>

The snoring of Winston pulls my attention to them, as I have found myself memorized by Emelia even sleeping. She truly looks like a sleeping angel. "Perfection." slips through my lips at a whisper. Slightly jealous of Winston and how close he is to her at this moment. Even though just meeting her, I have this gnawing notion that I have met her before. That I have known her my whole life without actually knowing her. Without thinking it through, I decide to lay down on the ground with both of them, on the other side of Emelia. Laughing in my head about when was the last time I slept on a floor. Last several years have been luxury hotel rooms or my own king size, pillow topped bed. I easily could have taken the comfy couch, but it was just as comfortable on the floor on a plush rug, plump pillows, and blankets. Careful not to touch her, I lay on my back, closing my eyes.

I'm awakened to sobbing sounds and a whining dog. Looking over, I see Winston pawing at Emelia's arm, as if to wake her up. I quickly roll Emelia over to her back, gently rubbing her face, asking her to wake up. With no avail and tears streaming down her cheeks, I decide to be more daring. Leaning down slowly, I plant a gentle kiss on her temple, then shake her arms a little. No change, as she lets out another whimper. Taken back by her soft, pink, full lips, I go in for another one, this time her lips. I know, I am a brave one. *Delicious, they taste like sweet honey.* This time, I am in shock to feel Emelia react to me, as her hand lifts into my hair and the other around my neck, pulling me closer in. Unable to bear it anymore, my tongue slowly slides into her mouth, and she lets out a moan that does me completely in making me hard. Our tongues begin to dance with each other, fully attuned with each other and wanting more. I roll over on my back, pulling her with me until she is straddling my waist. Winston begins to make his Chewbacca noises, as he's unsure what is happening in front of him. At that moment, Emelia opens her eyes, fully taking in who is in front of her and coming to the realization of what is happening.

"Oh my god…. Oh my god, did that just happen?" she asks, trying to regain her composure. I stand up in a flash to assist her.

"I am sorry, Emelia, not my intention to take advantage of you like that. It seems you were having an awful dream and crying, and nothing I did seemed to awake you. Even this big guy even tried." Pointing at Winston who is now standing under her, looking up at her.

Her face is blotchy from crying and if I had to guess, also embarrassment. Stepping in closer to her because her regretful face is breaking something within me, I lift my fingers to her cheeks to wipe the wet tears away, then place my hand under her chin to push it up so she has to look at me.

"Emelia, I am sorry. I figured even if I could startle you awake, you would no longer be in the nightmare you were trapped in, but then you responded in such an unexpected way… Dammit! Please say something."

Removing my hand from her face, and in a calm tone, she states, "It is fine, just don't let that happen again. I am not that type of girl, and you caught me in an emotional sleeping trance." She begins to walk away from me.

Hollering at her, I yell, "Can we talk about this? What just happened? Just slap me if that makes you feel better? What were you dreaming about?"

"Not that any of it is your concern, Lucas, but I have bad dreams often, but I am fine. As far as what just happened, I already told you. I am going to get dressed and head into town. Make yourself at home. Besides, you will eventually leave. Everyone leaves1" she yells back without even turning to face me and then slams her bedroom door.

Before I could think of what to say, she was gone from the room. All I can do is watch this dark-haired woman, with the tiniest freckles across the bridge of nose and deep amber eyes, walk away, while feeling a slight tug at my heart. Completely unsure of what it is or could be. I choose to give her the space she clearly wants and proceed picking up the living room and clearing away all the candles and items from the night before. Taking a quick look outside, it looks like the storm is slowly passing by. Just like the one I hence is brewing inside these walls.

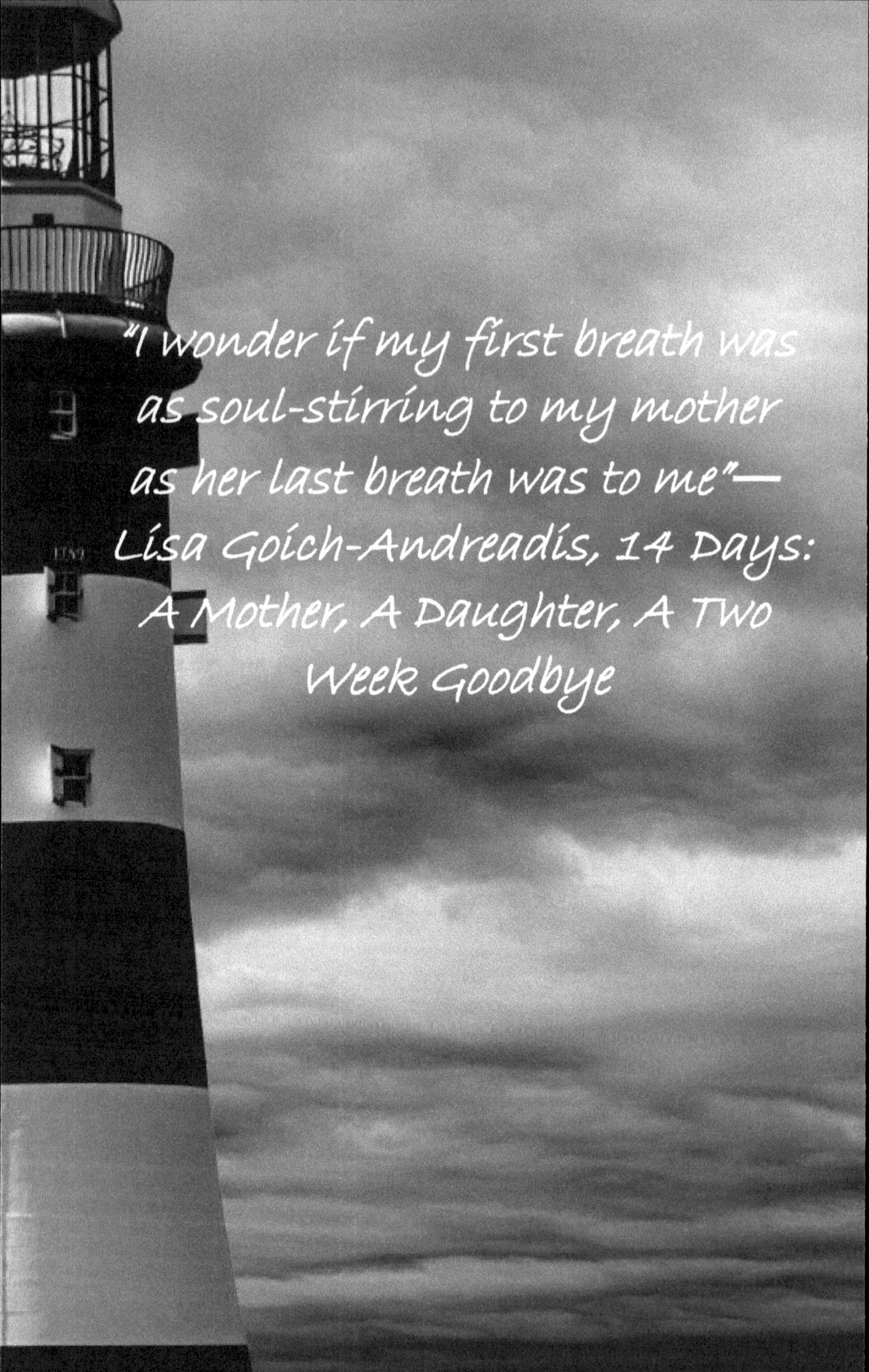

"I wonder if my first breath was as soul-stirring to my mother as her last breath was to me"— Lisa Goich-Andreadis, 14 Days: A Mother, A Daughter, A Two Week Goodbye

Chapter 7: Mama's Story

Mortification rides me hard as I run into town this morning. Running from him catching me in a weak moment where my body betrayed me. Running from my nightmares that plague me every night. Running as if my life depends on it.

How embarrassing it was for Lucas to have to wake me up from one of my many nightmares. But I am not really sure I can even call them nightmares. It was real life. It is my mind replaying that time in my life where my world started to fall apart. With my mama telling my sister and me that she was done fighting. With all hopes of a transplant off the table once she was diagnosed with Congestive Heart Failure on top of her end stage renal failure and you name it, all other issues in between, she was tapped out. Let alone home life was not the greatest for her.

Growing up, my mama was always sick. Unfortunately, her health downfall was tied to the birth of little ol' me. Nothing like living with the guilt of human failure all your life. While pregnant with me, she was also dealing with gallstones. Once I was born, she had surgery to have her gallbladder removed and a tubal ligation. In the midst of all this, the surgeon left some mesh inside her, causing a severe infection, leaving her ill and living off a feeding tube. Leaving me to basically be raised by my Granny for six to eight months of my life. No real mother-child bonding happening during this time. And where was Dad? Not there because he does not do well with hospitals or illness very well.

Mama survived round one. Fast forward six years later, we were on a family vacation in Galveston, Texas when she started feeling ill. A few days went by, and she could barely get out of bed to function. Mama had to go for round two, but it was the first time my mind memorized what it was like to see her be on her deathbed, while the Chaplain prayed over her. She ended up being there for months. At this point, Dad had already brought my sister and I back home to start school and make sure we were being taken care of. Leaning on neighbors and friendly faces. Mama finally flew home in early September, diagnosed with being diabetic as her pancreas was basically "eating itself" as she liked to put it. Over the years, there were a handful of more rounds that took her down. She seemed to have the craziest reactions to just a cold, multiple kidney infections and stones, high blood pressure, thyroid, and the list goes on. Just never ending.

When I was a senior in high school and my sister was off in college, Mama had seemed to have built a team of doctors around her by this point. One fateful day, she came home from her visit with her Endocrinologist, to let us know her kidneys were at a functioning rate of 30%, now officially giving her the diagnosis of chronic kidney disease. The doctor told her she had a handful of years before she would be at the end stage, needing dialysis, various treatments, and talks of a transplant.

In the middle of my twenty fourth year, Mama was fighting what she thought was a horrible sinus infection. Her body ached, even to touch her, she cried out in pain. Back and forth to the urgent care to get some prednisone shots and allergy meds, she only worsened throughout the week. Then my dad called me to come over to help him get her into the car so we could take her to the hospital. She was incoherent, slurring her words, she had no idea what day it was and was yelling in pain as my dad carried her to the car. By the time we got her to the hospital and rushed lab work, they were admitting her to the ICU. She was now in a comatose state, and we were unsure if she was going to come out of it.

I can't even remember all the numbers and lingo thrown at me that day. All I do remember is she was off the charts in many areas, and the staff was surprised she was still breathing when she came in.

Several days went by with my sister and I taking turns staying with her in between the dialysis treatments that were now being given. That might be round five or six at this point. When she finally woke up, it's the realization that the life she once had was about to drastically change. She got on a three day a week dialysis schedule, and doctor appointments filling in the other two days, luckily at least giving her the weekend to herself and time to rest.

Several months later, Mama fell and ended up fracturing her hip. My dad was out of town working, so it was my sister and I taking turns during her stay. I got a call the evening post-surgery from my sister in a calm panic. She and her husband walked into my mama's room only to find her face turning blue, not breathing, drooling. That the nurses were rushing in and out of the room, with "Code Blue" being shouted out over the hospital intercom. We stayed on the phone until the head nurse came over and said our mama was going to be okay. They had unhooked her from the vital machines as she just got back from the restroom and was eating dinner and had been doing well all day.

Well, the not so funny thing was, Mama was in a lot of pain from surgery and had been asking for "more of the good stuff" to help ease the pain and help her sleep. It for some reason did not register to anyone on-call, that all the anesthesia and medications given to her for the procedure and post had yet to fully filter out of her body due to her kidneys not functioning like a healthy human. To say the least, we could not wait to get her home, start physical therapy. and find a new normal.

A few more crazy instances, port surgeries, tethered nerve endings, more of her body failing in between then and the last incident that led her to her final decision. But during this time, she was on the transplant list, on a good routine for the most part. and had hoped for somewhat of a normal life once she received a transplant. My sister and I were never tested. Told we were not candidates before we could even offer, due to hereditary kidney infections and stones. The kicker was being diagnosed with Congestive Heart Failure and being told that the state her heart and body was in; if she were to undergo a transplant tomorrow, she would not make it off the table alive.

By this time, we were almost five years in on being on the damn transplant list, which was the ideal timeline if no one willing came forward to offer a kidney up, that one was soon to show up. She had already surpassed the lives of a cat at this point, but we felt she was such a fighter, and we would figure out a way and meet with her transplant team for options.

She was a fighter until there was nothing left to fight for. Yes, she had us kids and her husband. But she had also let us know a few near deaths prior she had made her peace with God. That she had raised her daughters to be the independent, self-sufficient woman she wanted us to be.

It was October when she landed in the hospital again. Dad was working hours away, and this time I had to break into the house as she called me stating she had fallen and could not get up. Upon entering, I already had an ambulance on the way. Nothing like sitting in the emergency room as tests are being run, only for a doctor to come in and go over all the drugs found in your mothers' system. Her prescription pain meds, Benadryl, aspirin, some other narcotic, and the list went on of prescribed and over the counter medications. Timeline was, she had dialysis on Friday, was home all weekend, skipped dialysis on Monday due to not feeling well, and now it was Tuesday evening. Trying to give my mama an out, but the numbers were still all too high and concerning.

My sister spoke to Dr. Mini, her pain medicine doctor and close friend of Mama's. She convinced us all that "intentional overdosing" had happened. That even though Mama had tried to hide it from everyone else, Dr. Mini stated she had been slipping in a deep depression for months now. Only the guilt reeled us in, to "How did we miss this?" and "We thought she was doing okay."

The doctor ended up admitting her to an inpatient stay for the remainder of the week. Several conversations were happening as we tried to look back on the last few weeks.

Her energy level had gone down, her legs were swelling more, and according to the dialysis techs, they were having to take more liters off her each time she came in. As Friday drew closer, we decided to admit her to a nursing rehab facility. Just for a few days so she could get her strength back, clear her system of all the medicine and get back on her dialysis routine. Needless to say, she was not happy about this. But we knew we had no other option. My sister lived an hour away, our "dear dad" was working counties over, and Connor and I had plans to head to Mexico for the week. Mama already threatened me not to cancel. Not sure about anyone else, but I always listened to my mama.

Plus, my sister was going to be staying nearby if anything was needed.

Nothing like getting the call, while trying to chill with a drink in hand. Mama had escaped the rehab facility and was at home. How? Even now, I laugh because that was all we could do during this time. Dialysis transport came and picked her up from rehab, took her to dialysis and waited for her to finish. Once she was loaded back up, she somehow managed to convince the guy to take her home.

To this day, I still don't have all the details of how she talked him into it.

But as he was driving her home, my dad started to call her, and she refused to answer. After several failed attempts, he called the rehab facility in search of her. They got back to him and said that she was supposed to have already been back at the rehab center from dialysis. Now they were trying to track down said transport guy. But In the meantime, Dad called my sister, who then started calling Mama, and she ignored her as well.

As transport and our mother got to the house, she realized she screwed up. She did not have keys or a garage door opener. She then decided to call my dad, and he found out what she had been up to all afternoon and now needed to get into the house. Dad talked to the poor transport guy and stated he could leave her there, he would be home in an hour.

Sitting around and waiting was not something she wanted to do, so she came up with an alternative way in, using the route of the broken window from when I had broken into the house the previous week. She legit had the guy go through the broken window, climb in and walk around to the front of the house to unlock the front door, so she could enter the house.

I honestly do not know what ever happened to the poor soul of a transport guy.

Upon my return, I found that conversations took place in the hospital with her Endocrinologist. Which boiled down to two options: One, keep on the path of treatments, take better care of herself, look to assisted living or in-home nurses so she was not at home by yourself. Two, dialysis was what was keeping her alive. She could end the treatment, and her body would go into a natural process of shutting down. End of.

After some deliberation of a timeline and holidays, she opted for ending treatment the Monday following Thanksgiving, and I would be home from college. Being that the plan was announced in mid-October, it became a waiting game, while we cleaned out the house and her closest, getting final paperwork in order, training on my dad's needs for his job when I was home on the weekends and casual conversations like death wasn't knocking on her door.
My laugh out loud moments now are when she was giving my sister and I her clothes she no longer "needed" but telling us which items to come back for after she passed because she needed to hang on to those certain sweaters for a couple more weeks, or me having to ask her to write down all her recipes since she wouldn't be around to cook for me anymore.

Who does this?

I only wish I could make this shit up! These are the moments I find myself laughing at now, instead of wailing about them.

Chapter 8: To Meddlesome

After doing a quick check on some neighbors and the library, I jog on the shoreline back home. Upon entering, I am elated to notice the power is already back up. I can hear the shower down the hall, so the need to avoid him is more evident. After I make a quick sandwich, I lead Winston outside to the back deck to take in the ocean breeze and the sun that is poking through the storm clouds. I'm going to soak up this quiet time before the rest of the week will have me spinning on my head. At some point I must have fallen asleep in my lounger, as I awake to my table umbrella shading me, the rest of my sandwich gone, *Winston,* and my sunglasses on the table with a note.

~Went out to run some errands and grab dinner in town. Enjoy the peace. Here is my cell if you think of anything you need. LS x

I check my phone to see it is already five in the evening and several missed calls from Mrs. Baxter. Even a text. As I open it, I am met with a picture of Lucas at *The Bistro* eating alone, with a message of, **why are you not here?** Bless it, that was just thirty minutes ago. I respond back.

Me: **Was taking a nap and busy. Why don't you join him?**
Mrs. Baxter: **Emelia, you need to get over here now, before you know which divorcee will snap him up! I can only keep the witches at bay for so long!**
Me: **Thank you but no need. Let them all have their fun. I am good here. Have a nice evening Mrs. Baxter.**

I refuse to respond to any more messages unless it's work or Summer Bash related. I head back into the house, feed Winston, then go take a shower. With my towel wrapped around my body as my loose wet hair drips down my back, I walk into the kitchen to turn the oven on to reheat my leftovers. While waiting, I grab a glass of sangria and stand there sipping, leaning more on my right foot, as my left leg is sore from my run earlier, just gazing out the kitchen window and getting lost in my own thoughts for a bit. It is funny...

"Uh-hmmm." The sound jolts me to turn around quickly, finding myself tightening the wrapped towel in my hands.

Our eyes lock, and he moves in steadily. The hair on my body takes a stand as he brushes his fingertips gently down my arm. Not once blinking or moving his forest eyes from mine. As if this moment will be gone if he does. I say, "I…. I… I'm sorry. Forgot I am sharing my house with a stranger… not like you are a stranger; I just mean I forgot someone… you were staying here and fell back into routine. Sorry. I am shutting up now…. Yeah … I am going to put some clothes on."

He quickly places his large hands on either side of the counter, locking me in my stance. It is now I notice; he does not have his sling on, and his wrist is no longer in a cast but just a beige colored medical wrap. His deep voice begins to pull me from staring at his freed arm.

"So, it's normal for you to walk around your house in just a towel?" he asks, smirking. "A little birdie told me you were going to join me for dinner, but I guess she lied."

"Are you asking or stating? And if it was Mrs. Baxter she lied, she tried, but I had things to do."

"Like taking a shower and walking around your house practically, *naked.*" Goosebumps prickle my arms as he whispers that last part in my ear.

Don't make eye contact, don't make eye contact, I keep internally whispering in my head. I move my hands up to his chest to push him back. *Bad decision!* He is rock hard, and my hands seem to wander on their own down to the etched abs I can feel under his shirt and back up again. *FUCK!* I look up to meet those damn forest eyes of his, that now have burning flames in them that match how the inside of my body feels. He slowly bends down, kisses my lips gently, then moves his lips slowly by placing light kisses all the way down my jawline, down my neck, to when he reaches the top of my wrapped towel. He looks up and is met with trepidation and want.

In one move, he lifts me up and places me on the counter. Spreading my legs wide enough so he can stand between them, making me aware we are more leveled now as we are face to face. "You know I can get you committed to hell with the things I want to do with you." My breath hitches as the pool of wetness grows under me as he keeps talking to me, touching me. Wanting him, like I have never wanted anything else before. "Darling, what are you doing to me? What is this pull between us?" he asks, pressing our foreheads together.

Wait. I know I have heard the line before.
Fuck, there is no way.

Pulling myself out of the trance he has me under, I put my hands on his chest. "Wait, please just stop for a minute." His brows furrow as he steps back perplexed. "Have you ever been to the Horse and Groom pub in Windsor?"

"That is a very odd and precise question. But yes, I live only a few blocks away, and I hang out there when I am home with friends." His body tenses and looks me straight in the eyes.

"Shit," we both whisper.

"You are the devil."

"You are the haunted amber eyes I could never forget."

"You could never forget me?" Now I am the one bewildered.

"Course. Over time your face became more of a blur, but your eyes haunt me in my dreams. I remember, I was drawn to you that day before I even saw your face, but as soon as you turned around on the bar stool to look at me, I was taken back. I knew I needed some strong lines to keep your attention."

"By telling me you were the devil and wanted to send me to hell," I gasp.

"It was to gauge a reaction. Your eyes looked deathly haunted and thought that might be my ticket. When I saw the flicker of light in your eyes, when I first spoke, I knew I had you."

"Had me? Who the hell are you? I have met some douchey men in my life, but never one as arrogant as you. Just so you know, I was going to decline your "sincere" offer, but you left with your friend before I could."

"Really?" he asks as he closes the space between us again. "What about now? Declining me now?"

"Yes, I actually am." As I step past him, I try not to let him notice me clenching my inner thighs together and head to my bedroom to dress. Calling Bec as I head out to the library to avoid my house with the devil inside.

Lucas's POV

For the love of insanity, this woman will be the death of me. I was surrounded by the women of the town all evening, nothing. No one caught my eye, no one seemed impressive enough to draw my thoughts away from her. Then I walk into her house and see her bent over the counter in a towel that barely covers her arse and leaving the long scar on her leg visible. It only intrigues me that I have caught her off guard, but I can sense her want. Even putting down a heater for qualifying, which is the most intense part of racing for me, my adrenaline and blood doesn't pump this hard. I am having to calm my own shaking, and I am not sure if it's fear or excitement that has me pulsing like this.

I am standing here in between her legs, letting her know how much I want her, how badly I want to please her, trying to control my own urge from flipping her over the counter right now and taking her from behind. Her sweet arousal is overwhelming my senses, luring me to taste her, to make her moan, to watch her succumb to pleasure.

"Darling, what are you doing to me? What is this pull between us?" I ask in a deep subtle tone, leaning my forehead against hers.

Then, BOOM! Like a missile penetrating its target and exploding, we realize who we are to each other. To her I am the arrogant devil himself, but to me, she is the vision of haunting eyes in my dreams. How could I forget those long dark waves down her back or those freckles that fall across her nose and under her eyes that are exaggerated by her full black lashes. Her streamlined flawless face that is topped off with her celestial nose and pink luscious lips. Literally, she makes me envision heaven and hell with her. The itch to be her savior, to love her, but the pleasurable heated hell I want to put her body through with mine. Just the need to be with her is overwhelming, and a feeling I have not had since the first time I met her. *Bollocks*! If only my mates weren't so pissed a town over and needing rescuing, I would have had my chance with her. But now that the fates have spoken; it seems only a night with her would not have been enough.

"Be worthy love, and love will come."
– Little Women by Louisa May Alcott

Chapter 9: Luck or Misfortune

Bec was no help with this evening's misfortune of me having to face off with the "devil." Anytime we have ever talked about him that has been the nickname we used. Now we have an actual name to the face, and holy shit, what is going on in my life right now? I need to wake up from this nightmare of a nightmare right now! I pinch myself. "Ouch," I yelp out. Great, still here, slamming my head back down on the counter. I literally have no one else to talk to about this. Not even Winston, who for one, I will not receive a viable answer back, and two, he has already betrayed me by liking the enemy.

Luck	Misfortune
Hotter version of Adam Demos (didn't think that possible)	He is the devil
His accent	He wants to take me to hell (what does that even mean?)
Second chance meeting (what are the odds?)	He is the devil but a handsome one

He is actually in my small town- in my house!	He lives in the UK - a bit far
Sexy and built by the angels	He is a racecar driver
Has the fates aligned?	Are the Greek Gods punishing him or me? Or both??????
I feel currents and fireworks between us	He is the devil playing mindtrick-eries with me
Everything about him turns me on	Like i said, a sexy handsome devil!!
He makes me feel, not alone	He will be leaving me alone

Just me and myself hanging out in the library alone right now. Pros and Cons list it is.

He will be leaving is about all I need to know to not even try to start anything with him. My body and heart have other plans it seems. My body yearns for his touch again, and my heart keeps calling out for him, as it is trying to break down the steel wall my mind worked so hard to build up. Damn you, Lucas Stratton, will you be my downfall this time around?

Lucas's POV

Well tonight has not gone well. Emelia left without a word, and I have no idea where she went or what she is doing. The thought of following her was great, but then decided against being that "Stalker" guy. I need to explain to her I am not this devil she speaks of, jokes of, or the womanizer bastard she has read about. Yes, I have been with plenty of women, but never been in a relationship, or been with the same woman more than once. Therefore, I have never cheated. We travel to towns and countries; I have my variety to choose from. Yes, I sound like a complete tosser. I am not a bad guy though, and I want something with her. It is way more than me just wanting her body; I want all of her.
It is after ten at night when I hear her set her keys on the counter. She spots me outside sitting under the streamed-up lights she has up. I motion for her to come outside, but she hesitates. I keep my gaze on her, keeping deep contact, before she finally starts walking my way, with Winston trailing her heels.
"Can we talk? And when I say that, I mean have a discussion like two grown adults that do not know each other."
"Okay, talk."
I move in closer, so we are facing each other, knees to knees. Taking a deep breath, I go all in.
"Tabloids are full of fake news. I will not deny I have had my fair share of indulgences, but not once have I ever treated a

woman wrongly or disrespected her. I have not been in any actual relationships with women to have broken any hearts. I have never used a pickup line on you that has been used on anyone else or can be found off the internet. Like I said earlier, I was gauging your reaction. If I had more time with you, I would have won you over with my actual charm and intellectual conversation. You would have known me because I wanted you to know me. That is something I never want. Women use me just as much as I have used them for a good time. There is more here than that. I know you are aware of this, and there is no way you can ignore it."

Taking a pause, I take in that she is more relaxed and hanging on my every word.

"I want to worship your body, Emelia, but only when you are ready. I want you wanting me as badly as I am wanting you. I want you screaming my name in pleasure," I murmur as I glide the inside of my palm down her face, causing her face to fall and melt into my touch. "I want to give you pleasure you have only dreamt of, more than you could possibly imagine. Most importantly I am willing to take this slow and get to know each other. I know that is so damn cliche, but I am not sure how else to put it."

"I'm not sure… not sure it's right for us to be together in any aspect. I am not the type that sleeps around and is used for a one-night stand. I also barely know you."

Looking back up at her, I shake my head. "You are not listening… I don't want you to do anything you are not ready for, but if you think you are just another fuck for me, you are mistaken. I am so drawn to you; it hurts to be away from you."

"Damn it! I am listening to you… I'm broken, Lucas. There is nothing good left of me."

I grab her face with my hands as I ask, "How can you say that? It's there, I can see it. Just like you can see me and not who you read about." I quickly bring her lips to mine and feverishly kiss her as she begins to cry. She is opening up to me.

Bringing her in my arms, I carry her to the couch and just hold her, kissing the top of her head and stroking her hair.

"When you hurt, something within me hurts," I whisper while rocking her to sleep, praying I do not mess this up as my complete Lucas Stratton aura fades away, leaving me stripped of any confidence or self-interest.

Chapter 10: Damaged Goods

I wake up in my bed with the light of the sun shining through my bedroom window. Apparently, a crying migraine is accompanying me as well, as I reference last night in my head. I quickly come to notice I am in my clothes from last night, but under the covers. Geez, I was such a girl last night, crying and falling asleep in his arms. *Who am I? Who is this guy that came out of nowhere over forty-eight hours ago?* Slowly getting out of bed, I go get dressed, brush my teeth, and put makeup on to cover the dark circles under my eyes. Today is a busy day, now that the full threat of the storm has passed, and we can clean up to set up for tomorrow night. Making my way out of my room, I am hit with the smell of bacon. Getting closer to the kitchen, I see Lucas in sweatpants and a t-shirt. His arm muscles practically have no room to breathe in it, but he is in my kitchen, cooking and singing with my Alexa. Winston at his feet waiting for a sliver of food to fall. This must be a dream, but a sexy one if so.

"Good morning, darling," he says in a cheerful tone. "You okay this morning?"

"Um, yah… I'm fine… Sorry about last night. It has just been an emotional and tiring week. The last thing I want to do is confuse you or think I am something that I am not," I say as I slide onto the stool in front of the kitchen bar. He hands me my tea, and I go to take a slight sip, as I'm not sure how it will taste, and he keeps throwing me off with this "darling" talk.

"Wow, this is really good. Thank you."

"You are welcome. You know… I notice you and all that you do."

"I can see that," I snark, lifting my mug up in the air, silently congratulating him.

He soon places a plate in front of me with eggs, bacon, and avocado loaded toast, then comes around to sit next to me.

"This looks delicious, but you know I am the one that is supposed to cook for you as the host."

"I think we have passed the line of host and guest, don't you?" he asks as he looks into my eyes, and for the first time, I sense he can see into my bare soul. I quickly tear my eyes away from his.

"Emelia, about last night… I need you to know I meant every word. You are not a conquest. I know this seems fast, but there is this magnetic pull to you that I can no longer ignore."
Sliding into a trough of panic, I slam my fork down on the plate. "What is it about me that you think you want?"

"Why do you think that way? Who hurt you so awful that you feel you do not deserve to be loved, to be treasured?" I can tell his temper is rising by the veins in his neck, and he keeps clenching his hand closest to me.

"It is just that everyone leaves, they always do. And you will too. You have a whole career that takes you all around the country, the whole damn globe. So why would I allow myself any happiness or pleasure with you to be left and broken again? I just met you *Again,* and you have already turned my world upside down. Seriously, what is to become of this? Of us? You get me for the summer then leave, go back to your life before me. While I am still here, only alone again."

"I can't give you sight into the future, Emelia, only the now. Why can't we see where this goes and figure out the rest later," he sighs "Trust me not to hurt you."

"I do not know you, Lucas, let alone enough to trust you with my heart." I spat out through my tears.

"Dammit, Emelia. Then know me! I am asking you to fucking know me. I am not one who has to beg for what I want, but I am begging you to talk this through with me. There is something unexplainable between us, you yourself cannot deny it." His chest heaving in eagerness, as he pulls my hand up to cover his chest where his heart beats fast.

"There is a static when you are near, since the first time I saw you, I felt it. I don't know how to be in a relationship, but I want to give it a chance with you. I want you to let me in, into your mind." He taps my temple with his long index finger then drags it down gently to my chest. "I want you to let me into your heart. Please, Emelia. Fate, the stars, God, whatever in the literal hell you want to call it, has brought us back together. This is no longer a coincidence." Emotionally exhausted and feeling this is a battle I am not going to win at this very moment, at least while we share the same roof, I can at least admit he does have some valid points. What are the odds we were to meet again, let alone the very first time? "I… I… I can try." Holding my hand up in front of him, I stop him from getting too excited. "Everyone closest to me has left me in some form, so I keep my distance from others to avoid heartbreak. I am broken, Lucas. I do not trust easily, I overthink everything, I shutdown if pushed too hard. This is me letting you know this will not be easy for us, especially for you."

Pulling me in his arms then kissing the top of my head, he says, "I am just asking for the chance to put you back together. To be the one that makes you happy for however long we have."

All I can do is nod my head against his chest, as my heartstrings feel like they are being pulled down into the pit of my stomach, and I need to brace myself for when they snap.

Lucas's POV

As Emelia curls up in my arms, I wonder who I am, and how I got here. I know I am a thirty-four-year-old handsome–in my eyes–male, from Berkshire, United Kingdom. I had a good childhood with two sisters and loving supporting parents. They worked hard and always supported my need for speed and to be behind the wheel of anything I could drive at all stages of my life. The most rebellion I had was in my twenties when I was thrusted behind the scenes of the racing world full of travel, fun, and women. Lots of women. I cannot even say it was truly rebellion but getting lost in the thick of it all. So yes, the many articles of me have me surrounded by the ladies, a different one at every event, showing what a good time I was having.

I have not once thought about settling down let alone being in a monogamous relationship. Until her. Until I laid my eyes on her from around the corner. Her amber eyes looked broken but with so much desire and love to give. Her midnight hair waving down her body to her mid-back with the most innocent angelic look I have ever seen. She has haunted my dreams for over a year now. Even now, her energy is pulling me in toward her, her sinless look asking for someone to save her. I feel that someone has to be me.

As far as my race career and how I ended up here in the small-town Rhode Island, I was recently signed to the American GT series a few races in of the season and right before the British Series began. I was driving an Ace of a car, the McLaren 720S in the GT3 British series and now will be getting behind the wheel of a McLaren 720S in the GT4 American series. My long-term goal has been to be in Formula One racing or Indy, either on the McLaren or Ferrari team.

During practice two months ago, the axle of my left wheel broke, causing the car to catch, sending me spinning until the left side of my car slammed into the barrier. It hit so hard, splintering my wrist as I did not have time to let go of the steering wheel and popping my shoulder out of place with a slight muscle tear. The pit crew got an earful from me and the team owners, *damn dipsticks*. Knowing I would not be ready for the April and May races, it was a decision to move me over to the American series that has a break between mid-April to June. The McLaren team wants to capitalize on the American tracks and win, and since the other guy drives like

Latifi in F1, constantly spinning out on his own, the owners feel this will be the best move for now.

Flip side of that to being dropped into a secluded little town; it is all about keeping my playboy self out of trouble. My agent knows anytime I have, I spend with my boys, and we always have a way of getting ourselves into heaps of messes, or as I like to explain, trouble has a way of finding us. So, to be safe and being kept out of the limelight while healing, my agent found this quaint town, and all I have to say is, it must all be fate.

Now I am starting rehab three days a week for my shoulder and wrist and hitting the gym the other two. I was furious when my phone alarm went off earlier, alerting me it was time to leave to get to my appointment. I hated to leave after I just broke through some barriers with her as she seemed calm. Knowing I will see her in a few hours to help out with the Summer Bash set up helps ease the blow. Until then I am going to let this bloke get me in shape. Need to make sure I look my best for Emelia but also ready to get back behind the wheel of the racecar.

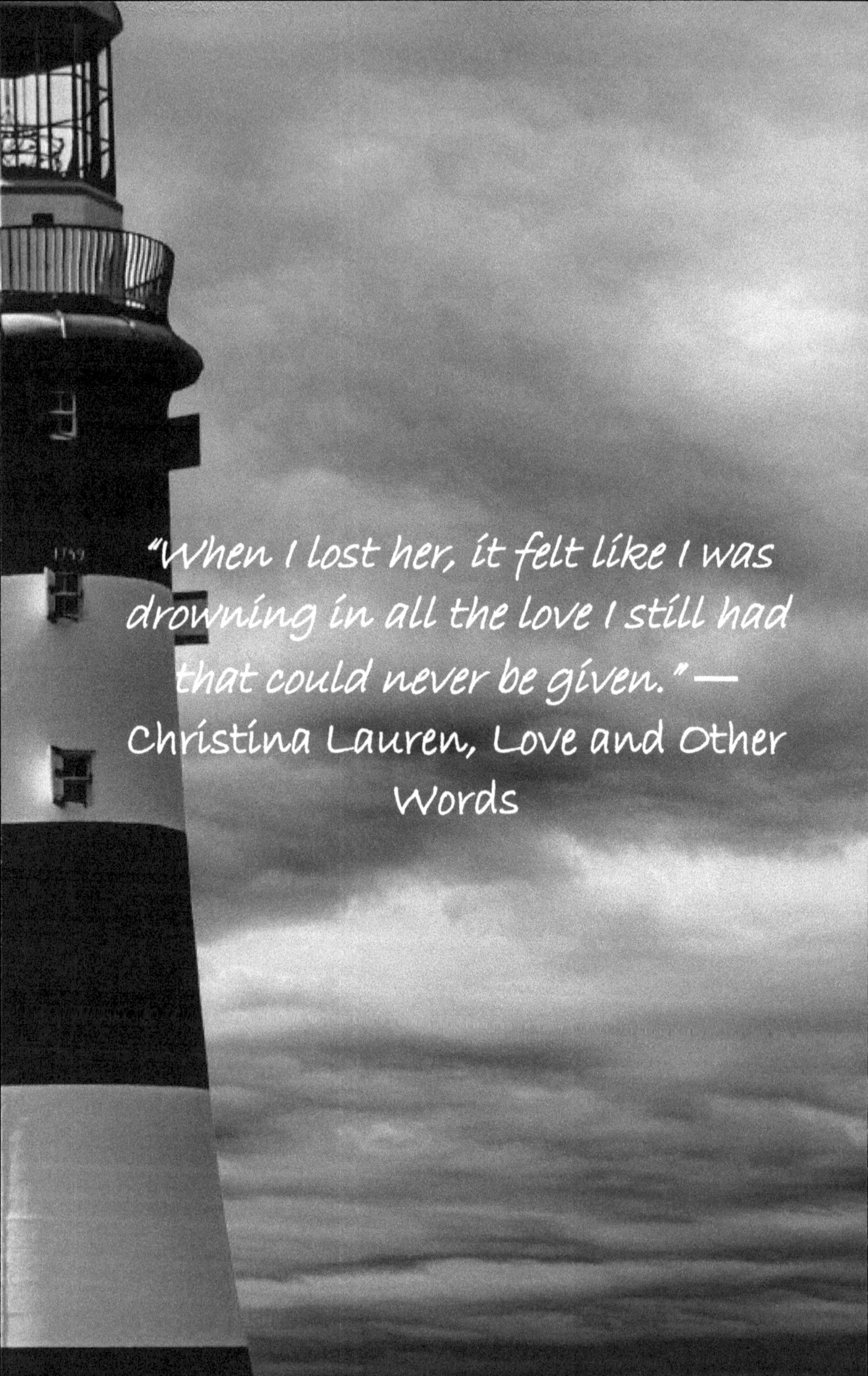

"When I lost her, it felt like I was drowning in all the love I still had that could never be given." — Christina Lauren, Love and Other Words

Chapter 11: The Show Must Go On

After an emotional overload within the last twenty-four hours, I am happy to be out here on the beach, with the sun finally pushing its rays through the gray clouds, busying myself with layouts of tables, bonfire build, catering details, and decor. The weather is supposed to be perfect this weekend to celebrate Summer in our quaint town. This time of year has always been my favorite. Now maybe more than ever because of the memories and comfort it brings me. I used to perform at this shin-dig with my dance studio, and my mama was always in the front row cheering me on.

During college, I always made sure I was home in time for us to spend this day together and hang out. Checking out the old and new vendors, making sure we were first in line for the fresh chocolate covered popcorn and cotton candy, as well as catching up on the latest town gossip. Over time, it was more of me pushing Mama around in her wheelchair, as she no longer had the energy nor would her body allow to be-bop in the midst of it all. In hindsight, I really wish I would have known that that summer would have been our last one. I would have made sure we really indulged in all the goodies and hung out until the fireworks lit the sky. Instead of letting her talk me into taking her home early so I could enjoy the rest of the evening with Connor and friends. She always felt she was a burden no matter what I said or my attempts to prove otherwise. She was my person. The person I called first thing in the morning; She was who I called on my way home from work and usually we chatted before bed, if I was not already over there for dinner.

I honestly can say, even after years have passed, she is the one person I'm still unsure how to do life without. The one thing she had always told me is no matter what else is going on, "The show must go on." Cliche, I know, but it resonated with me. Not just on stage but how I approach life. Life keeps going regardless of if I or whomever else needs it to pause. How life pushes us to find our own moments of peace, whether it be on the cold tile floor of the shower crying our eyes out or sitting in the car ten extra minutes to get yourself together before walking into a house of people that need to *think* you are okay. My favorite may be the midnight ice cream binge while looking through old photos and calling her number over and over again just to hear her voice on her voicemail.

When Dad decided to disappear, the option of hearing my mama's voice disappeared with him. He canceled their phone plan, and I lost my mama's voicemail for good. I was wrecked for days.

Followed by the angst behind not being able to follow up on the promise I made to Mama. To keep an eye on him, to check in on him and make sure he was okay. In a matter of days, I spiraled so fast into a despair of darkness, I blamed him for her being gone. That he pushed her to the point of leaving us behind, like she had no other choice. Pissed that I knew he loved her but never fully gave her the life she deserved, and then the infamous affair with the bitch, Sheryl, in the town over.

Even in the end, Mama wanted to make sure I looked after him. She loved him; she also resented him, but she loved that man. Who am I to fault who anyone loves in this world? The older I got, the more I threw myself into romance books, believing that there is a soulmate for everyone. Maybe multiple of them, depending on place and time. Believing that love was to happen when you least expect it to, that fireworks would blast through the sky with the first kiss, butterflies in the pit of your stomach existed with just the thought of that person. I came to believe that there is someone who truly loves you for all you are, brings out the best in you and makes it a life goal of making you happy and content. Sure, there are life struggles and decisions in between, but when the fates align correctly, it all works out, *right?*

Can't say I had the fireworks with Connor, maybe a few butterflies, but he did make me feel appreciated and respected. A sense of security, but he even took that away not too long ago. Lucas, on the other hand, makes the hair on my body stand up, as if I am being electrically charged when he is near me. I could almost swear I heard fireworks off in the distance when he first kissed me and every time after. He is fighting for me, even though he doesn't know me. He wants me just from being in my presence. He wants to fix me, regardless of how shattered I am.

Of course, I swoon over this man I have known all of seventy-two hours of my life, but he acts as if he has known me his whole life. The fact he reads me like a plot in a book, getting every twist and emotion right should be unsettling, but honestly, I find it comforting. Comforting in the fact that I do not always have to explain myself, and he knows when not to push me. Lucas is always watching me, taking all of me in, hoarding questions in his brain until he feels I am ready to answer them. My guard is up, but he somehow is slowly chipping away at my steel harbored wall.
Getting through my own thoughts, I turn to look behind me as I can feel the electrical current running through my body, sensing him somewhere nearby. Spinning around to search, I quickly spot him standing by the bonfire area looking in my direction. I just finished sketching the table arrangements and adding all the names to the seat placement cards in calligraphy. As much as this is a non-formal affair, the classy townspeople love organization and seeing their name written out and placed before them. No one tends to argue this, so I make sure we do it every year. Even for the kid tables.

Needless to say, thirty minutes after everyone eats, chairs are pulled up to other tables, kids are running around everywhere, people are playing in the water, as well as the drinks are pouring. Sometimes we are graced with the presence of a few celebrities that spend their summers with us. I like to think they enjoy the idea of normalcy; because to this town, they are just another person the people want to share historic facts, old fishing stories or talk about traditions and family with.

"Hello, darling," Lucas mumurs as he leans down to kiss my cheek. "I figured I would help with the bonfire build, unless you need me elsewhere."

"I think that is the perfect place for you, but please be careful with your wrist and shoulder."

"Yes, ma'am. I promise to be careful."

"Smartass!" is all that seems to fly out my mouth, causing him to chuckle next to me.

"I do have an important question for you though."

"Uh-huh," I answer as I look down at my checklist.

"Can I take you on a proper date this weekend?" I slowly look up, meeting his intimate gaze. His eyes seem more of a sun-filled rainforest green today than the intense dark forest I have been getting lost in.

"You serious? A date, out in the town?"

"Well, I figured it would not be too much of an issue being it is only inevitable, plus the town is already talking about us anyways. And being that I really like Mrs. Betty down at the bagel shop, I would like it to be in her favor of winning the bet."

"A bet! A bet about us?" I ask astonished.

"Yes. I hear the pool is up to $2500.00 now. The bet is when we have our first date. Everyone had to pick a date and then a time spot. Mrs. Betty's bid is this Sunday at seven o'clock, give or take thirty minutes."

I am rendered speechless at this point. I start looking around at everyone, only to realize everyone is looking at us.

"This is ridiculous!" I exclaim, throwing my hands in the air.

Mama's words register with me, *the show must go on.* Last spoken to me two days prior to her passing. Taking a deep breath, I say, "Yes."

Lord only knows what I am getting myself into. Lucas kisses my cheek then makes his merry way down to the bonfire build, leaving me pondering on what is happening in my life right now. I feel like I am staring in the latest rom-com book waiting for the disastrous scene to implode.

Allowing myself to imagine what a future with him would be like, as I see he fits in this town and my life so well, so easily. But deep down, I know this won't be our future. That there is no future with him. He has a career that will pull him from my world for several months at a time. A dangerous career where anything can happen out on the track, even when all safety measures are met and whatever cautious mindset you can find going over 190mph. The ending of this will be more like the Titanic, but I will be the one sinking to the bottom as Lucas stays alive on the floating door.

Chapter 12: Summer Bash

Bec gave me a pep talk earlier this afternoon about enjoying this for myself. That I just go into this with no feelings, and if I develop *said* feelings like we already know I have, then take it that I am not completely dead inside. She did promise to murder him though if he completely breaks me. As she ended the call with, "drink up bitch and let loose." God, I wish she was here with me. This is the second year they are missing the bash due to schedules, and it will be another month before I see them. I did get to enjoy the vendors with Lucas some before having to prep for the evening. Us fighting over the last bite of cotton candy as he chased me down while I shoved it all in my mouth seemed to be a nice spectacle for the crowd today. Then we attempted to try every twenty-one types of mac and cheese from the Big MAC food truck before feeling completely sick. Lucas even talked me into making our first sand art piece together which ended up being a *very* colorful masterpiece in the shape of a dolphin that he plans on placing on my fireplace. He let me know he had not been to a festival or anything like this since he was a kid, so he made sure to experience everything today with or without me when I was pulled away to deal with an issue or answer questions. The last time I saw him was over an hour ago when I left him with the house husbands' drinking beer while keeping watch on the kids in the moonwalks.

"Hey, my darling. Can I help you with anything?" Lucas asks as he comes up behind me, chasing me in circles. People are already arriving and have changed into their evening wear and dinner does not start for another half hour.

"Can you just make sure all the tablecloths are tight and secure and …" Before I can finish my sentence, he is holding me in bridal style. "Lucas, what are you doing? I need you to put me down. Like right now."

"I can't do that…. At least not until you take a seat and delegate."

"Why would I do that? I have a thousand things to do in a matter of minutes."

"Because you have already thrown your shoes off. I see you leaning against everything you possibly can to take the weight off your leg, yet running around here, chasing people and things down without any thought." I can only stare up at him because he has been watching me so intently this whole time. Even when I thought I had him busy enough with other things to keep his distance from me. "When was the last time someone took care of you? I mean really took care of you, Emelia?" I can only shrug and look back down at my checklist. He carries me over to a chair, placing me down.

"I am fine, really, Lucas," I state as he grabs my clipboard from me.

"Emelia, these items have been checked off a thousand times already. Are you just trying to keep yourself busy? Busy from me?"

Feeling the heat rise in my neck, I quickly turn to him. "No, it is my system to ensure things are done. To check them a trillion times before I am comfortable with it being complete." I begin to glare at him while holding my hand out, so he returns my clipboard back to me.

He slowly does. "Okay, I believe you. I have to say though, just looking around and looking at your many check marks, there is nothing else to do. So let the guests come down and get this party started." Nodding my head, he signals at his right-hand man for the day, Oliver, to break the rope and allow people down the slanted walkway that leads down to the sand and lit up tents.

All I can do is let out a little giggle as Oliver has been attached to Lucas all day, and not once has Lucas complained or showed any sign of annoyance. After promising him to take a five minute break, he goes off to help guide people to tables, and I jump up to oversee the catering set up as soon as I think he is not looking in my direction. Only to soon get the intense glare from him from across the way as he guides Mrs.

Baxter and the widowed group to their table. I give him a wink and turn back around to my task, taking advantage of him being occupied.

This year has the best menu yet. It is one we have not done since my mama passed. One very long, extended table has a cajun low country boil spread out across it with all the shrimp, crab, potatoes, sausage links, and mini corn on the cobs you can imagine smothered in butter, onions, and cajun seasoning throughout. Another table is done up with fancy shrimp cocktails and truffle frites with all the sauces and dips aligned across the white and gold table runner. Then of course a full wide salad and raw oyster bar followed by the extravagant dessert table full of decadent mini cakes, chocolate chip vanilla dipped cookies, hazelnut mousse along with my favorite, mini apple tarts provided by *The Bistro*. All the food is under wide white open tents streamed with firefly lights through and in between them all. We have four open bars scattered through the area so no one should wait too long for a drink, as well as many servers tending to the guests. The dance floor has streamed lights above, lighting up the space with the moon as it rises. It truly is a remarkable sight to see up against the water's edge.

Everyone is eating, drinking, and enjoying the festivities. The high class seem to be content with all involved as well as the generations of townsfolk. Even for me, I find myself stuffed with delish seafood and salad. As soon as I think my drink is empty, the glass magically is full again. The waiters are on it this evening making sure no one goes *thirsty*, tonight. Though I will admit, it is probably not a great thing for myself. I have not drunk this much since that one dreadful night. Since the night of the accident–I should remain thankful I am alive, only a few scars to remind me of my decisions, of the spiral I let get out of control–I barely indulge in one glass of wine or whiskey. Now I am sitting at a table with the summer elite, trying to track the conversation happening before me. Catching up on their lives from over the year, since we only see the majority of these families through the summer, sometimes in the spring as well. Nodding when I feel it's needed along with keeping my ears perked for anything that is directed to me to answer.

Soon enough though, I feel the electric current pass through me as I feel him come up behind me, then I feel as he places his left hand on my right shoulder, giving it a slight squeeze. Attention is suddenly on him, and as if he was there to save me, he whispers in my ear, "Here, take this water and go freshen up. I got this." All I do is nod in acceptance then politely excuse myself from the table, taking the cup of water Lucas hands me. I quickly down it on my way to the ladies' room off the pier.

A few passes through the crowd to ensure all is good and everyone is having the best time, I find myself down the beach, near the water's edge, sitting back on a lounge chair. Sitting, I feel like I can finally breathe and take in the appreciation of how tonight turned out. Looking over at the party happening to my right, I see all smiles, all happiness even if a few show it for these several hours only. The generations that have passed through this town, have shared their neighborly love and care down to their kids and grandkids and so on. I see the young and old out on the dance floor all dancing together like one large family. It is a sight to see every year. Also, one that makes me miss partaking in. It was my dad who danced with me when I was little, my mama that watched me when I got older, and then Connor who spun me around and proposed.

Such lighthearted memories that now only bring me to painful tears. I quickly wipe my cheeks for any escaped tears, as I feel a presence coming up behind me. I do not even have to look behind me to know who it is before he even speaks.

"Emelia, I have been looking all over for you. Are you doing okay?"

"Yes, I am fine. Just taking a breather over here. Trying to sober up a bit." I let out a hiccup followed by a giggle.

Taking a seat next to me on the lounge chair, leaning back, he looks over at me. "Aren't you a petite, cute drunk." He gives me this cheek-ish grin that only makes me smile more. Yep, all the alcohol has kicked in, another reason why my emotions are everywhere. Suddenly, Lucas easily and quickly picks me up, setting me on his lap, so I am now facing and straddling him on the lounger.

"Now this is a much better view," he says, running the pads of his fingers along my face and through my hair. With the feeling of liquid courage to back me, I take his face in my hands, pulling him to my lips. A whimper escapes me as his tongue starts to dance with mine. His hands reach for the back of my head, pulling me closer into him as we are feverishly kissing. Both letting out slight moans of delight and desire, letting our fireworks shoot off to the sky. I soon feel his erection through his pants against my heat. Being that I only have a sheer layer of lace panty between us as my dress is hiked up to my hips, it overwhelms my core senses. My body reacts to his engorged length, and I begin to grind against him as I can feel the intensity build between us. He is holding my hips tightly in his hands, pushing me down on him, as we find a grinding rhythm together. His one hand lifts and slowly enters the top side of my dress, finding my breast to fondle and tweaking my nipple for extra sensitivity as we grind harder against each other. I pull away from his mouth to sit down harder against him. He lets out a groan that rivets through my body, making it want more.

"Bloody hell, this feels incredible. Give me your mouth back!"

Leaning back down to him, we wildy keep kissing, clashing teeth as if we can not get enough of one another. The wetness between my thighs is growing, and I seem to have found the perfect spot where his erection is grinding along my clit and down. I start to feel my body tense, as he pushes me down harder on top of him.

"Lucas, I..I am going to… come. I can't stop…please don't stop what you are doing!"

As if on cue, his hand drops in front of my abdomen, slowly gliding its way between us to my core as two of his fingers begin to circle my clit as he pushes up against me. I moan loudly into his mouth, grasping his shirt and skin as I come undone.

"Fuck, Emelia… come on, come on, darling."

I finally feel my whole body convulse, releasing a pent up orgasm. My grinding slows as my body comes down from its high. I feel and hear Lucas do the same, gripping my hips tightly as he pushes me down on him. He grinds against me three more times as his eyes roll in the back of his head, and he almost falls limp with exhaustion.

Silence falls as we continue to look at each other. Lost somewhere between extreme lust and what the hell just happened? Then sudden realization of where we are. I quickly shoot up, looking over to the party, but it seems to be going on as normal and none the wiser that we were over here having dry sex like two sex crazed teenagers trying not to cross the taboo line.

"Come on, let us walk back up to the house to get cleaned up, and then we can rejoin the party," he says as he carries me piggyback up the dunes to my house. My face bent down in his neck, inhaling his bourbon and woodsy scent, bringing me to a calm place.

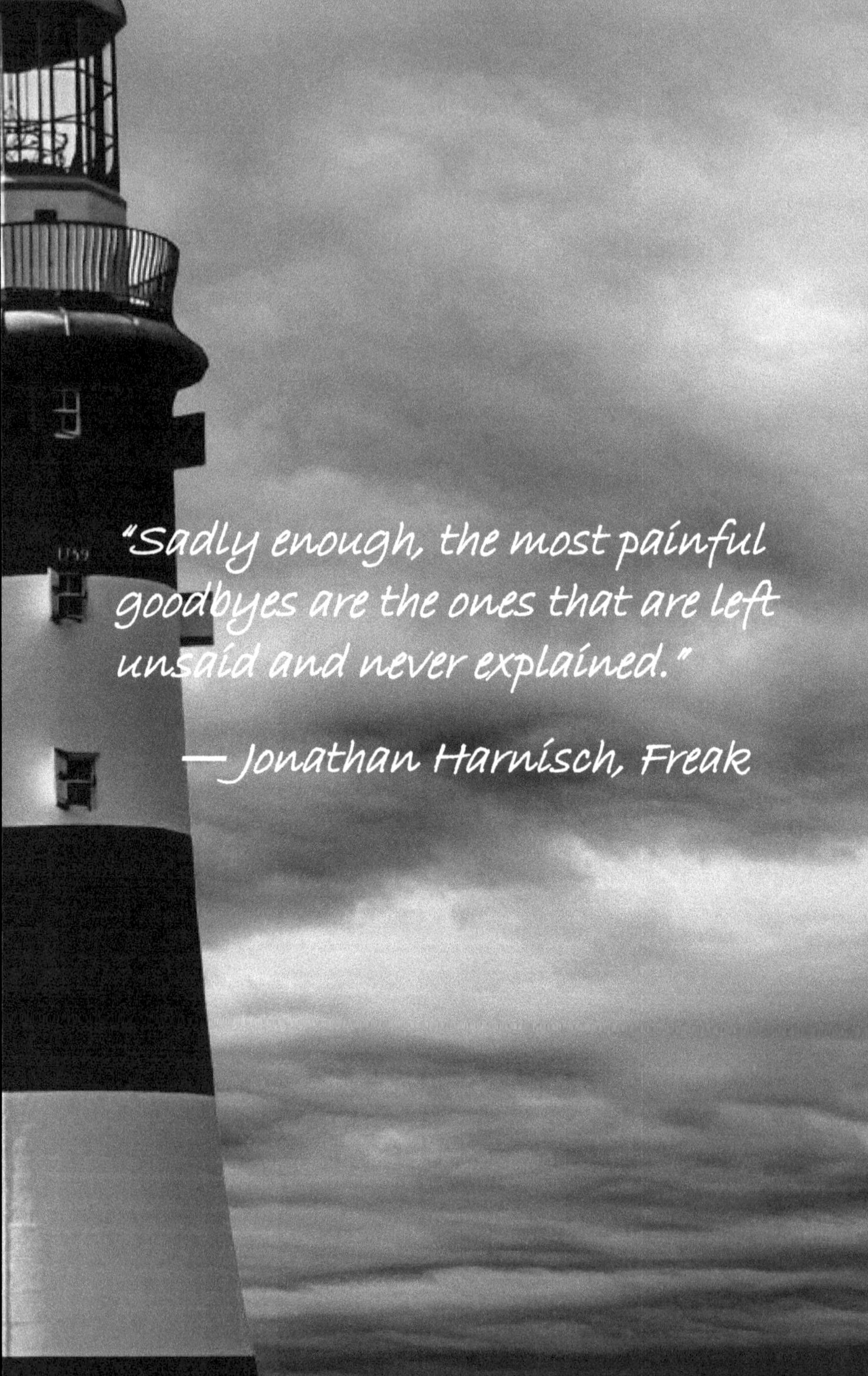
"Sadly enough, the most painful goodbyes are the ones that are left unsaid and never explained."
―Jonathan Harnisch, Freak

Chapter 13: Induced to Speak

Several more rounds of mingling, more drinks, and hours later, the summer bash party finally is dying down. Kids are passed out in lounge chairs, even a few laid out on towels in the sand. Covered in head to toe of sand. Laughing to myself about the hassle the parents will have getting them awake and cleaned up. There is the drunken party crowd made up of returning college students for the summer, all playing catch up and have started their summer hangovers. The highschoolers that want to hang with and be the college kids have their own spot by the bonfire. I enjoy watching the small, separated groups of cliques amongst the middle schoolers that act too cool to be at this small town party, but secretly enjoy being part of this tradition. The much older crowd has already returned home, and the middle-aged crowd is a mix of those wanting to pass out from the continuous partying and those still holding strong. Mostly the men of the group, as the women, especially the moms, look at their sugar comatose kids, trying to figure out how to get them home as well as their befuddled husbands.

Now pushing midnight and the breakdown crew just arrived, I give the staff their directions, and they maneuver through the remaining crowd to start consolidating and packing up. All the leftover food is getting packed up to be delivered to the on-call law enforcement and medics in town. Lucas has been great with helping with the breakdown and checking on me by a hand touching my back or wink with his passes. An hour later, all is packed up, and Marcy is off to deliver the leftovers. Lucas grabs my hand, walking me down to the water's edge, sinking my toes in the wet sand. I slowly lower myself to take a seat in the sand, as he rolls his pant legs then takes a seat next to me. He wraps his long arm around my waist, pulling me closer to him.

"What now?"

"Usually, I stay out here until the sun rises, taking in the quiet and beauty of this end of the island in the early morning. Sometimes I get lucky and see the dolphins playing and chasing the shrimp boats as they head out for the day. Catching the cranes and beach birds fly over as they start to find breakfast."

"You able to stay awake for that? I can see your pissed eyes."

"Pissed?" I ask, looking up at him confused.

"Drunk. I see your drunken eyes," he laughs as he smiles at me.

"Using your slang on me, got it." I straightened my back, cracking my neck to the left and right.

"Not going to lie, it has been a minute since I have had this much alcohol in my system. Drinking here and there is something I do, and I love my evening wine at sunset, but not like this."

"Is there a reason you do not, let's say, indulge in it anymore?" Unfortunately for me, the alcohol, especially lots of wine clouds my emotional wall and inability to lie or hide things. I try to look away, only for Lucas to grasp my jaw with his good hand, making me look back at him. "Come on Emelia, give me something…. Give me something, and I promise to give you something in return."

With a sigh, I relive the night of my accident in detail. Connor had just left to head back to Boston after an awful fight we had. He did not say it outright then, but I knew it was the end of us. It was not even that I was upset about my fiancé leaving, but the fact that one more person had left me. That all the despair and heartbreak I had from my mama's passing was surfacing. All the fury, hurt, and annoyance from my dad's disappearance was rearing its ugly head. Every damn emotion I had been suppressing over the last few years started to pour out of me that night. I had wine earlier at dinner with Connor, probably one to many already that led to the escalation of our fight.

What started the fight, I have no idea. What it ended up being about, was me being a bitch and not agreeing to move back to Boston with him. Once he left, I opened my dad's leftover bourbon and started pouring and throwing back.

Trying to drown the pain before it could resurface, but at the time, it was lost on me that I was losing that battle by a long shot. And I mean several shots later, I was sitting on my back porch contemplating my whole life. The good, the bad, the love and sadness. That my sister and I were a product of love, but several years in living in this fucked up life that at the time we thought was normal. Normal for parents to fight, normal for our dad to have a girlfriend in the next town over as our mom was buying time through the years. It was normal for him to buy a car and gifts for *her*, when there were times we thought we would lose the house after pulling a second mortgage on it and our very own livelihood at stake. Normal that every time Mama ended up in the hospital, he ran to that woman's arms for comfort, leaving his daughters behind to comfort themselves. So normal, that he would come home and have conversations about her with his own wife. A woman that wished my own mother dead, so she could have my father to herself after twenty plus years later.

I look up at Lucas who has a tense jaw but is holding my hand through all this. Taking in my every word, like he does not want to miss a detail of it. Continuing, I let him know I am past it all now, but yes, there was a time I did not want to deal with the pain anymore. To feel like such an outcast in this town, in this family I was part of it. Because I felt everything I ever knew was a lie. That love was a lie. That anyone that thought they were in love were delusional sick fucks who were blinded by their own selfishness and greed. That no one was truly capable of having a love story. My parents did not have one, my sister was saying she was happy, but I threw her quickly into the delusional bucket, and apparently, I myself was not meant to have a love story as I knew Connor and I were over.

So as I swung my legs over my back deck rail, now with a bottle of gin I was trying to finish off, and in the midst of all my thinking, I closed my eyes. Closed my eyes to think I need to push through this, but also question was it worth it all. No one would miss me; I was sure my dad would be notified and would come back to take over the house. Probably with the bitch Sheryl. Sure, the townspeople might miss me, but they would quickly find a new librarian, and Mrs. Baxter and the bridge club would need to take back over the island's festivities. I must have been talking to myself for a while because I heard Winston start barking, so I quickly opened my eyes. Startling my own self, I was dizzy and felt very off balance with blurred vision. Dropping the bottle, I recall it hitting the sand below me. Again, feeling off balanced but furious at myself for dropping my bottle below, my dumbass instinct kicked in to look down. At that point, I tumbled over, somersaulting all the way down. My leg somehow landed on the dunes fence post, causing it to go straight through, shredding the skin and muscles in between. Fracturing my femur. As my upper leg was caught on the sharp fence post, the top half of my back and neck landed on the gin bottle, shattering it with force.

"Shit, Emelia. Your deck is at least twenty-five feet off the ground if not more," Lucas astonishingly states. All I can do is nod.

"Definitely not my proudest moment, but luckily Winston's incessant barking alerted the neighbors. The Masons."

Lucas quickly puts the two together. "That's Oliver's parents."

"Yes, his parents found me, called an ambulance as his dad, Jake, wrapped and kept pressure on my leg. At that point, we did not even realize I had shards of glass in my back or neck. That blood loss was realized once they cut the fence post so they could take it with them to have it surgically removed at the hospital, but they had to lift me and carry me to the back of the ambulance. Of course, this is also all based on what I have been told; I was pretty much in and out of consciousness at that point. I am told once they got me to the hospital, lots of imaging was completed. Then I was put under and through surgery. First for my leg, and then to extract the glass from my back and neck." Looking at Lucas, he is standing up now, pacing between the chairs. "I know it is a lot, but I also told you I am broken. Though I am in a better place, the pain is still there, from all of it, from the loss of everyone," I whisper the last words as a tear creeps down my cheek.

"What else?" he asks.

"What do you mean, what else?"

"I can tell there is more." Looking out into the dark abyss of the ocean and sky, I try to find peace to tell him more. When a slight breeze blows through suddenly, I know what I should do.

"Here, take my hand and follow me." He quickly does quietly.

We walk up past the pier and a block over. There to greet us is a tiny seashore vaulted cemetery. I refuse to look back at Lucas, but I feel him squeeze my hand a little harder as we walk through the gates. I lead him through the mazed path that goes up the hill. I drop his hand to pull out my phone, turning on the flashlight, pointing it at the headstone. The headstone that sits beneath a carved statue of a baby being covered and forever shielded in angel wings.

I hear Lucas reading out loud to himself. "*Here lies Baby Greer, though I have not met you, I love you. Though I have not seen you, I dream of you. Though you are gone too soon, you will never leave my heart. My forever angel, Love mommy……April 2021*"

He stands there in shock, speechless, just staring at the headstone, as if reading it repeatedly was to make it more real to him or something.

"After a few good days being awake and calm, the news was broken to me that I was two months pregnant. But due to the impact of the fall and the trauma caused, there was nothing that could be done to save my baby. The worst thing is I didn't even know. Connor and I rarely were sleeping together, though I tried to appease him when he came to visit. To not want to lose the one person I had left in my life. We were always careful though, so it was a tragic miracle in itself."

Calmly and with a darker tone in his voice he asks, "Does Connor know?"

"No… No, I never told him. He was informed as to what happened and came to see me in the hospital. By the time he got there, he was cleared of any link or medical access to me, so he only knows what I told him. I do not plan for him to ever know. Because I know Connor enough that he will feel obligated to come back, take it as a sign we are to be together, and try again at building a life together. Which is not what I want at all. There was never a heartbreak or sadness when he left me, it was the feeling of being alone again I did not want to handle. So when I say everyone leaves, I mean everyone leaves me."

We are only a few feet away from each other, but it takes seconds for him to reach me, wrapping his arms around me. "My darling, darling Emelia. I want to kill that ex for you, track your father down, bring him back begging and screaming for your forgiveness. Most of all, I just want to hold and love you. And if you allow me to do just that, it will keep me from seeking revenge on those that have hurt you most." He lifts my chin as he leans down, giving me the most perfect kiss under the moonlight.

All I can do at this point is tear stain his white button up Armani shirt and collapse in his arms. Strong arms that I was not aware I needed in such a dire way. A way that gives me hope to be happy. Maybe it is the reason I have been looking for to exist.

Chapter 14: Pick a Date

It is six-thirty in the evening, and my room is a disaster from the tornado of clothes that has ensued over the last hour. I finally settled on a turquoise halter dress, giving in to my hair's natural waves and light makeup.

Knock, Knock

"You know this is like the third time you have knocked in the last hour?" I yell out through my door. "Just five more minutes."

"You said five more minutes thirty minutes ago, Emelia," he conveys.

I slowly open my bedroom door, revealing myself to him, as his eyes take me in from head to feet. Clearing his throat, he says, " I have to say, the wait was worth it. You look divine, Emelia."

Every time my name rolls off his tongue, the heat grows through my body, and it truly makes me feel special. Important to someone. To him. My eyes are locked on his deep forest gaze. Taking a deep breath, I break our stares to step past him to grab my sandals by the door, trying my hardest to pull my steel wall all the way back up, so I may enjoy this evening, enjoy being with Lucas, but without my heart getting involved. My heart cannot fall for this man, I know this much.

His palm gently lays on my lower back as he walks me out the front door, down the steps, and over to his red fancy sports car. After opening the door for me, he places a kiss on my temple, then he holds my hand as I slip into the passenger seat. Once settled, he shuts my door, then walks around getting into the driver's seat. Looking at me, a smile overtakes his face. "You ready?"

The way he asks leaves me to believe he is not just asking if I am ready to go for a ride, or on a date with him. A sense of him asking if I am ready to fall for him, to be with him. The answer is clearly a *no*, but all I can do is nod my head yes. My body is tense, and my mind racing about our intimate moments, the laughs and conversations we have shared over the week. As I gaze out the window, I feel his large, gentle hand on my thigh in between shifting gears, trying to tell me it will be okay. That I should not be fretting over something so common as a date.

It's something people do constantly, whether something new or established. For me, this is new. New on so many levels since being alone for so long, the electric current that flows between us that provides so much intensity, it makes me fearful for my heart. We are like magnets being pulled together, and I'm not sure how much longer I can resist his voice, his laugh, that smile, his sexy olive skin toned body. Resisting him alone has become a daily struggle for me. Though he gives me space and respect, it's the little touches that spark between us. It is when he says my name in his British accent that makes me swoon, how he and Winston have come up with their own schedule for walks and play, how he is not overbearing but looks after me. How he is just here. *Here*. That word that stands out in my thoughts the most.

Lucas's POV

I took her to the Ocean House for dinner, and we enjoyed dinner outside while the ocean breeze kept us cool. She finally seemed to relax halfway through our meal, but I know she is still holding back from me. Especially since I saw a whole other side of her on Friday night. Granted it was wine induced, but she was cutting up, laughing, flirting, grinded against me till I literally came in my pants - *an experience I have never had or expected*, and let me in for a fleeting moment. Long enough to hear about her accident and the loss. Long enough to let me see her shield down and the pain she possesses.

Looking at her now across the table, she is brimming with life and desire. Always taking in her surroundings, thinking. The sun is hitting against her side and back in just the right spot where it looks as if she is glowing. Her amber eyes have sparks in them since I first met her. Her hair now pulled in a loose bun on her neck so it's no longer sticking to her neck and face. Now I can take in her long sensual neck at a better view, and I can adore those freckles on her face without her hair whipping around her face, blocking them. *Shit!* What has happened to me?

I am so immersed with her. Losing my self-control, my thoughts are only of her, even when I am at the gym or on a virtual track racing, trying to remember every bend and turn I need to prepare for. My sense of self is changing, as if there is another purpose for me. That the purpose is her. I have had a good life with the want of nothing. My parents were strict but loving. My siblings, my biggest fans. Sure, I went to church, but will probably burn in hell for the sins and acts I have committed against the holy book in my adult life. The only aspiration I have ever had since I was a young lad was to be a race car driver. To be an international race car driver for either Ferrari or McLaren. Everything up until 8 years ago has been to earn my place amongst these teams and drivers.

Eight years ago, I began the journey to keep my place amidst the rankings and to be at the top. Kent probably called at the perfect time this morning stating they need me at the Virginia Speedway by the end of next week. A few days there to test and practice since my surgery. Then I can come back and not due out for another two weeks for another run, and then we pick up every weekend until race week. Seven more weeks until race week. I can do this. I can balance my time with her and the track. I must because the thought of losing her scares the shit out of me. I also know being signed to the American team in the interim until the start of next year's GT British Series is a big deal. One I cannot afford to lose my head or arse on. I honestly do not know how she is going to take the news, and I keep waiting for the perfect time to break it. I guess it is now or never. Dessert has arrived, and anyone can handle all news well with chocolate mousse pie, right?

Taking a bite of the pie, I say surprised, "You were not lying. This is an incredible pie."

Smiling, she murmurs, "I told you. I am not sure you will find a more delicious, melt in your mouth, gooey, succulent pie around."

"Agree." Take another bite. "By the way, I heard from Kent today."

"Oh…I am sure he is ready to get his favorite driver back in the tabloids." She smirks.

"You have jokes, I see," I say in mock-offense, letting out a chuckle that allows her to give me back one of her lustful playful smiles. *She can throw jokes at me all day if it gets her face to light up like that every damn time.*

"So what news did he have for you?"

"It looks like practice is about to start up, and since I get released from therapy in two weeks, and I have met all my physical and fitness goals, they want me in Virgina at the end of next week." She nods, and I can tell her wheels are turning. "But it is just Thursday through Sunday, then I will be back. And then just every two weekends after that until race week."

"Oh, that is cool. Well, I am sure you will be happy to get back behind the wheel on an actual track. I hear you yelling at that video game constantly."

"Video game?" Not sure if I should be offended or laugh at her. "Video game it is not. It is a simulator. Made to make you feel like you are actually in the car, driving the track. Learning all the turns, straightaways, when to break, and when to gas. It is amazing what years of technology has given us to have this insight prior to just hitting the track at first practice. Especially for me, never been on American tracks."

She gives me a nod in understanding, still not making eye contact, so I give her a minute to process all I have said, before speaking back up.

"Look, I know it may be too late of a notice for you to come out next week, but I would really like it if you could pick a weekend you are willing to be there." Emelia now looks up at me with those amber eyes that seem to have a wetness to them now.

"You want me to fly out there and watch? To visit you?"

"Yes, I do."

"Okay. Just pick a date and I will be there."

"Really?" I question, almost astonished she agreed so easily and did not just cut me off at the limbs. She looks back at me like I was crazy to question her. Then I tuck this moment in my memory, knowing I must keep learning all sides to her and how to read her completely. "Okay then, I'll book you a ticket for the second weekend of practice. You can fly out Friday, and we can fly home together on Sunday."

The rest of the evening goes way smoother than I anticipated. I even overheard her telling her best friend, Becca, about it and seemed genuinely excited. I have also come to terms that this Becca friend is another person that is in line in front me along with Winston. Along with the fact I am already terrified of this friend, based on what Emelia has told me and her threats. Emelia showed me a picture of her thinking I would remember her, but she keeps forgetting the only person I was looking at in the pub was her. Yes, her friend is pretty, but my only type is type Emelia.

"She took a step and didn't want to take any more, but she did." — Markus Zusak, The Book Thief

Chapter 15: Slow Dancing with the Moon

It is Wednesday, and the week has been going by so slow. Maybe I should enjoy the slowness of it since Lucas will leave Thursday evening. Sure, he will come back, at least that is what he says. He also handed me a first-class ticket to Virginia so I can join him in a couple of weeks. His agent Kent flew in last night since his Airbnb magically became available early. After Mrs. Galant and Mrs. Baxter dropped by Monday morning to share the news, I was shocked to hear it was available at all.

Those two sneaky women are always up to something in this town, and it's just my luck that I am their secret and master match-maker plan. Being that it is only a few doors from my home and in walking distance on the beach, I guess they felt we would be okay having our own spaces back, after being thrusted into each other's lives this past week. I won't lie though, as much as I know not having him around constantly will take some adjusting, I am looking forward to having my space back. As I keep my steel wall up right, it will only make it easier when the time comes for him not to return. So as Lucas and Kent get situated over there this afternoon, I have another routine day at the library.
From my Bluetooth, over the shelves, as I put up the last books of the day, I hear my favorite song come on. Dolly Parton's *Slow Dancing with the Moon.* The lyrics have stuck with me since I was a little girl. I was always the one talking to the Man in the Moon at night. Telling him my secrets and silly crushes to, discussing life choices with, and dreaming with him. Hell, I still do. The Man in the Moon is who I cry to. It is he who has always known me best, and I like to think with all the moon phases, my own life has aligned with them, to him. Other than Winston, it is him that has heard my anguish cries of longing and despair of loss. Now swaying and singing with the lyrics, I find myself reminiscing even more of the innocence of my childhood and young adult life. When life was simple and easy, well easier than it is now.

Easier than when all hell broke loose upon me waking up to come to terms with my dad's affair, thinking most of my childhood was a lie I fantasized about, and Mama's diagnosis. How much I romanticized life, the reality I had for myself and my future. But then the second verse flows into the chorus, and it hits me like a dagger, and I stop moving.

Somehow my heart never grew up, no one ever burst my balloon
So here I am swirling in star dust slow dancing with the moon
Still believe someday my wildest dreams will all come true
And I'll find someone who'll make me 15 again
But until then I'm Slow dancing with the moon
Oh, the stars got in my eyes long time ago
And I've lived my life like a love sick clown In a bittersweet cartoon
Just a dreamy-eyed kid slow dancing with the moon

As I cling to the lyrics, I realize that I am no longer that girl. Someone, something did burst my balloon along the way, and I have lost that starry eyed, adventure seeking, dreamer of a little girl. The parts of me that were happy, lived to love, and loved to live. *Damn.* The realization of that girl gone, and this woman I have become is a heavy relief almost. Like recognizing this hard truth is something I needed to do a long time ago. I have loved, I have lost, I have endured a tragic accident that should have been all so life changing, but only made me realize I am not capable of keeping anyone with me, but to cut back on drinking and depression. To go back to harboring my feelings and emotions because losing myself to them only leads me into a dark abyss that I may not survive the next time. That there needs to not be a next time.

This is life. Life is not fair, but I do not think it is meant to be this cruel either. The knowledge that I have been dealt a grim hand of cards in this life, gives me hope that maybe my next one will be wondrous, and that the one before this had to be everything I have ever romanticized and felt in my soul. For now, I make the decision to live my life as I see fit, until my purpose and time is up. Because that is all I can do, instead of drowning in misery.

I am standing at the last shelf I got to when I look up at the line of books to figure out where I need to place the next book that remains in my hand. I laugh out loud. *O fate, you do have a sense of humor.* I stare at my personalized romance shelf, starting with **The Thorn Birds,** running through Jane Austen novels, a touch of Edgar Allen Poe, and of course **Dante's Inferno** with **Wuthering Heights** and **The Great Gatsby** in between, then fading into my favorite new age romance authors. Where my deep love for reading romance began to where it is now. It almost looks to be a timeline of how characteristics of love have changed, how love is shown and depicted. The one thing these all have in common, is the heart wants what it wants. Whether right or wrong, villain or hero, received or lost, love is not temporary, regardless of what type of love it is. I glide my fingers over the edges of the bindings down the line, until I find the perfect spot for the one in my hand. **Over the Moon, by Elissa Haden Guest.** My teenage self devoured this book over and over again. Happy to see a new generation reading this. I push the book in where my classics end and my new age begins, signifying the shift of reads.

I turn the corner to be welcomed by a wiggly Winston and the handsome, beaming face of Lucas.

"Big boy wanted to go for a walk, which then led us here. So can we take you to dinner?" His smolder makes my knees buckle, so I steady myself next to the end of the shelf.

Smiling, I reply, "Of course. Let me just put these back over here and lock up." He lets Winston off his leash so he can follow me around.

"You big bear, come on. I think I have some treats behind the counter for you."

Lucas helps me close, and we head off down the path with Winston leading us. Pretty sure we are being led to the hole in the wall sandwich shop off the beach. One we frequent quite a bit because the company is great, but the food is mouthwatering. I can already taste the lobster sliders, but starting with smashed avocado toasts laid in bacon, red pepper, and avocado on slices of toasted French bread. I wipe the side of my mouth, already salivating over the thoughts of food. Lucas catches me.

"Already drooling over me? We are just getting our evening started."

Shaking my head, I try hard to hold my laughter in. "Just ready to put my mouth around something flavorful," I say in a sultry tone as I give him a wink. I am returned with a wide-eyed look, but he soon stops me, blocking me in between him and the brick wall of a building. His tall stature towers over me, and he gently grips my chin, lifting it up so my lips meet his.

It is like a forest fire in his eyes, as he speaks, "My darling, look at you being a tease today. Be careful what you wish for?" Then he lowers his mouth for a kiss, a deep one. One that strips the breath from my lungs. I can't even gather my words to speak, to say I was talking about the food Grabbing my hand, we continue down the path, trying to catch up with Winston who did not stop for us, as his nose is on a mission. A mission for bacon.

Lucas's POV

I have barely touched her since Friday, trying to give her space to soak it all in. Sunday night after our date, I gave her a good night kiss after we hung out on the back porch following dinner. Telling her about my life, likes and dislikes. So, she can know me. Though these talks have been merely touching the surface of who I am, I know she needs surface before we go deeper. She needs to trust me, though I tell her repeatedly I am here for her. That I want to fix her broken heart and dreams. That something bigger than us has placed us together. She jokes about it being the old ladies of the town, but I sense she also experiences the same electrical currents when we are in the same room. The same shocks and sparks when we touch. She nearly jumps in her own skin when I touch her. Not because she is scared or it hurts, but it resembles a jolt to the heart. I know, I feel it every time too. Though tonight, she seems lighter, assuaged even.

We have just finished a true mouthwatering dinner, and now we are hanging out at the bar, watching Winston strut around the place, making sure everyone acknowledges him and hopefully shares some of their food. I am going to miss not being in the same house with the big guy. He gives the best hugs and always has me laughing when he demands Emelia's attention. Whether her attention is on me or other things. Then they have their own parent- child hollering match for five minutes before all is calm in the house again.

"Haven't asked how you are doing today. You seem different than this morning when I left."

"Um, I had a moment today that allowed me to discern a few things I have needed to process for a while now. Allowing myself to feel much lighter now with good headspace. Hey! A few more of these you might even get lucky tonight."

"How do you do that?"

"Do what exactly?

"Take a thoughtful moment and spin it into a joke or a ruse. Is that a gift you have?" I ask, perplexed.

She meets my glare. "Not a gift I am aware of. And sorry if I do that more than I realize… It is one of my coping mechanisms. But seriously I am good. Whether it is timing or a mixture of things. Thank you." She places her hand on my knee, and with an imploring gaze, she leans in to kiss *me* this time. I take in her soft lips tasting like her cherry bourbon drink. Grabbing her head, stealing one more from her.

"Thanking me for what?" I ask as my forehead leans against hers. Keeping her close, I allow her scent of honey, paper mixed with leather and bourbon to overtake me.

She speaks softly, "Thank you for being with me. Whatever this is between us, I appreciate you taking your time with me and understanding. Shedding some light in my dark world." I can't help but lace my fingers in her dark waves and pull her lips to mine. Crashing together, all sense of where we are is gone. This woman is making me lose myself all over again, as her tongue intertwines with mine, her hands around my neck and in my hair. I pull back slowly, biting her lower lip before pulling away, but my hand's still entwined in her waves of hair.

"What are you doing to me? I want you so bad, Emelia. I am waiting, but damn, I need you to know how much I want to taste every inch of your body and put myself inside you. To feel you lose all control with me. Not to pressure you, but so you know. So, there is no question in this head of yours."

She nods a yes in between the palm of my hands. Our gaze breaks by a demanding Winston.

She yells over to the bartender Stacey to get some drinks to go and throws cash on the bar before I can even reach for my wallet.

"It was I who was treating you tonight." She puts a finger to my lips, hushing me.

"My treat this time. You have done enough." Grabbing our drinks from Stacey, she turns to me. "Let's get this grumpy bear home for bedtime. We can walk on the beach and take in the sunset on the way."

Our hands wrapped together, we head to her place, and in that moment, I observe her walls start to crack, and even a few pieces fall when I look in her eyes, that now resemble a brightening golden sun.

Chapter 16: Test Time

It is Thursday evening, and Lucas just left for his track weekend. I am trying not to fragment into pieces. To push myself these next few days. Marcy is covering the library tomorrow and Saturday morning so I can start planning for Blues on the Beach on Wednesdays and Friday beach movie nights for the next two months and fourth of July. We have several local bands already booked, but I need to circle back to my vendors and decorator. Make sure the fire station ordered enough fireworks and not just the holiday knock-off ones they attempted to set off last year. *Gosh, what a disaster that was!* Luckily Oliver's dad and the police station had a surplus of the big fireworks. The fire station was put on the town's "ignore" list for months until they begged and groveled. I think the kicker was when they almost burned down their own station trying to cook an actual meal, instead of being fed by the love and kindness of thou neighbor. Even with a heavy to do list, my mind goes back to Lucas. No, I did not throw my body at him for a final attempt to keep him here. But we did have a pretty spectacular makeout session when he left my house last night, and then another one this afternoon before he left for the airport. His kisses and touches were full of promises and passion. That is what I have to hold on to the next several days. He said he would call when he landed and would reach out as he could over the weekend. That the weekend will be packed with testing, schmoozing sponsors, and team, along with getting a feel for the car and track. It is not lost on me that he belongs behind the wheel of a race car. I have spent much of my spare time this past week googling him, his stats, his British team, and now his American team. Watching old races and championship videos. The ones where champagne is being sprayed everywhere, and he is having to stand there taking a million pictures with different sponsor hats holding trophies. Being lifted up by his pit crew and team, smiling from ear to ear the entire time. It was probably a bad idea to tag his name to google alerts. Because it seems the world has taken notice of where he will be this weekend, but I do not take for granted that no one knows where he has been hiding. My best kept secret from the rest of the world, and what I love so much about this town. That if an outsider was to find out, they would be chased out with pitchforks, literally. Winston joins me on the window seat, and I know he is missing his buddy, so we give each other extra cuddles and kisses. Falling back into our routine, but with a little more pep in our steps. *Emelia, you got this! Just 3 days, and he will be back here with you. Deep breaths!*

Lucas's POV

I just landed and got off the phone with Emelia before I even disembarked the plane. She seems to be okay. More than okay actually, and I am honestly not sure how I feel about that. For me, I felt my own withdrawal as soon as I left her standing on her front porch. As I looked in the rear view of my car, she stood there with a smile on her face as the ocean breeze whipped through her hair. She had no makeup on today, just so I could adore her freckles and kiss them. Her golden eyes shining back at me is a vision I long to keep and see when I close my own eyes. It is late when we get to the hotel, so I send her a text. **I already miss you - LS x**

I should have known better that that woman never sleeps. Her mind is always racing when she is awake, and the fear of what dreams will take over when she does sleep.

Emelia: **We miss you too! x**   *Attached is a picture of her and Winston on the window seat.*
Me: **Get some rest, darling. I will reach out when I can tomorrow. LS x**
Emelia: **You too. Good luck tomorrow and be safe. A -x**

It is after two in the afternoon before I can even reach out to Emelia. It is just a quick text letting her know I have been up since five this morning but saw an incredible sunrise on my run that made me think of her. That first round of the track was alright, but we need to tweak the car some more. I do not bother to go into the details and technical terms of it all. I would rather show and explain when she is here with me.

The rest of the day is spent completing mock runs to collect data, then reviewing with my race engineer, Lorenzo. After dinner with the team, I hit the pillow so hard. Jolting awake at three am, I feel like something is wrong. I look at my phone to only see a missed call from Emelia a few hours ago, but no other messages other than one from my mum checking on me. I make a decision to call Emelia back. The phone just rings and rings on my end. Still feeling angst, I hang up and call back. Finally on the fifth ring she answers.

"Emelia, are you okay?"

"Lucas?...hey…what time is it?"

"It is a little after three. Sorry, I must have woken you up. You can go back to sleep."

"No, it's fine. Everything okay on your end?"

"Yeah, it is. I was knackered when I got to my room earlier. Sorry for not at least texting you. A very long exhausting day. Ready to be back with you."

"Mmmm, that sounds nice. Can't wait…. Oh wow!"

"What is it?"

"Nothing, I am just now fully awake and realizing I am covered in sweat. No big deal. Guess I will go and take a shower."

"You were having a nightmare, weren't you?" It goes quiet on her end.

"Darling, answer me please."

"Yes, just the usual. Nothing I can't deal with."

"Well, go take a shower. I think I am going to do the same, now that I realize I am still in my clothes from today after leaving the track, plus have to be up in two hours. I will call you after my run, okay?"

"Okay. Thank you for waking me up I guess." She lets out a slight laugh followed by a hesitant shaky sigh. "I am okay, really. I will talk to you in normal morning hours. Night, Lucas."

She hangs up before I can say anything else, but let it go. For me, I am wide awake with the part of not only covered in dirt and sweat myself, but that frightening fact that I felt something was wrong. That something told me she needed me even being hundreds of miles apart. I bound into the cold shower to relax and calm down as I feel amped up for all the wrong reasons.

I called her after my run, but no answer, and so I head over to track for breakfast and testing. Walking into the trailer, my cell vibrates. Pulling it out of my pocket, it's from Emelia.

Sorry I was still sleeping. Have a great test day. See you tonight! A -x

Shooting one back quickly, I see the team owner approaching.

Glad to hear. Thanks. LS x

As soon as I am off the plane, I am full on sprinting to get to my car. Leaving Kent in the dust, knowing he needs to grab the luggage and another way back to the house. Speeding back to Watch Hill, I pray I do not get a ticket. Surprised I take an hour drive down to forty-five minutes, because right now every minute without her hurts. As soon as I am out of the car, I turn to find her at the top of her porch, waiting, staring as if it really is me. Soon she skips down the stairs, running then jumping into my arms. I place one hand under her bottom, as my other pushes her hair behind her ear, then pulling her into a gentle kiss. A gentle kiss that turns heated, and she has me carrying her back up the stairs into the house. Shutting the front door with my leg has our bodies slamming into the wall in the foyer. Both hands everywhere, desperate for closeness, needing each other. No words are needed by her when she gives me my answer with her blazing amber eyes.

"If all else perished, and he remained, I should still continue to be; and if all else remained, and he were annihilated, the universe would turn to a mighty stranger." — Emily Jane Brontë, Wuthering Heights

Chapter 17: Calling Out

For the love of all things holy! It is eight in the morning on Monday, and after last night and having to call Marcy to open the library, there is a good chance I will not be making it in today. Luckily being the awesome human she is, she doesn't ask questions or thinks twice about it.

I am in the midst of making my English tea in the kitchen as he comes rolling out of my bedroom in just his Calvin Klein boxers. *Lord help me!* His leg muscles bulge out of the dark blue material. His boxers hinged on his hips as my eyes trace down his stomach to his *V* as his light happy trail of hair dips into them. His messy hair has a *just fucked* vibe as his eyes gaze imploringly at me while he saunters to where I am behind the counter.

"You snuck out of bed, my darling," he whispers in a gravelly tone as he grabs my ass, pulling me into him.

"I need some caffeine and just called out of work for the day," I say with a smirk then take a sip of my tea.

"Damn, it is already past eight. I feel like that is something you typically do not do, am I right?"

"You are right. But being that I waddled to the kitchen like a penguin this morning, my neck, chest, and arms are covered in bite marks and bruises along with every muscle in my body aching, it seemed like the best decision." He chuckles, but then soon lifts me up, placing me on the countertop and begins to inspect his doings.

"I am sorry, darling. I did not mean to harm you and intensely ravish you so hard."

"You did," I say, smiling at him. "And it's okay. Can't say I didn't ask for it and even begged for more." Leaning in to kiss him on the cheek, he plays with my hair as it intertwines in his fingers.

"Last night was incredible, Emelia. I have never experienced such a raw, emotional, and intimate moment. With you, that is what it is, every. single. time. Please tell me it was the same for you. That I am not alone on this island when it comes to us."

Taking a minute I ponder what he said, because in hindsight this has moved along so much faster then it probably should have. I also can't deny the unmistakable connection between us. The electric current that flows between us is effortless, overwhelming, and all too consuming. *Watch your words, Emelia. You are happy, and you are making strides to change yourself. Don't mess this up!*

"It was. This is… This is all crazy and incredible. I will admit we fit. We fit in the most surprising ways." Thinking to myself, *from my hand in yours to your length inside me, to your mouth on me.* Our personalities are in sync. I feel a smile grow on my lips.

"Earth to Emelia. You have a look of wickedness on your face. Please do explain yourself." Damn his accent and precise formal way of speaking. Makes my breath hitch every time. It may be my own illusion as he makes me feel I am living a more passionate Jane Austen novel.

"I got lost reminiscing of our dirty deeds from last night that carried over into the early morning hours, and how truly well we fit together." I enforce my innuendo by giving him a wink.

He quickly lifts me to where I am straddling his waist as he carries me across the house, back to my bedroom.

"Let us continue our dirty deeds then." Throwing me on the bed, then stepping out of his boxers, he is all kinds of sexy. What a specimen of a man, and my eyes refuse to look elsewhere as my body pulses for him. He then begins to strip off my t-shirt and lace panties, making his way between my thighs. Kissing, sucking as I arch off the bed as his tongue licks between my folds. Hands now clenched into his dirty blonde locks, I begin to buck as his tongue darts in and out of me as he slips two of his fingers inside me. Curling them in and out of me as the pressure increases. I call out his name as

I come undone against his mouth. Him not leaving any wetness between my legs before he climbs up over me.

"Can we just stay here in bed all day?"

"Yes, my darling. Yes, we can," he murmurs as he begins to plant kisses down my neck and onto my chest. Guiding himself into my entrance, we begin again. And this… this is ecstasy.

Lucas's POV

Bloody hell, that woman. She is my beginning but will also be my end. At least that is how my lower member and body perceive it to be. We spent all morning and afternoon in her bed. Rolling around, devouring her, and just talking. She is starting to know me. *Finally.* I need her to know me and trust me. I know we can be so much more when we get to that level. Strange coming from my own thoughts. Not once have I had a serious girlfriend or wanted one. Right now, I am doing what just feels right in the moments as they come. No holding back. Not even knowing if that is the best thing to do or not, but we are making this work for *Us*. She spoke some more about her mum and childhood. We talked about our favorite books and movies, and now I think I will be stuck in an eighties rom-com movie nightmare this coming weekend. To see her smile though, I would walk through hell's fire for it.

I even noticed a fancy photo box sitting on her dresser with pictures of her and her mum. Asking her about it, her eyes went wide, when she sees it in my hands.

"Lucas, I am going to ask you to slowly put that down, and when you do, I will tell you." I do as she asks, putting it right back in the spot it was, then looking back at her. "That's my mama." My turn for my eyes to pop out of my head and panic.

"Um… I thought there was some weight to it, but it seems like a pretty intricate photo box."

"It functions as both. No need to panic, but that is where she is."

"Do you plan on keeping her here, like always?" I ask, concerned. My family buries people. I have only ever been to funerals where people went in the ground, six feet deep in the ground, not burned and kept in a box.

"Not sure. My dad was supposed to keep her but asked me to hold on to her. I think he felt too guilty to have her around, even though that is what she wanted, along with being buried with him when he dies. I do not even know where he is at this point. Um, the second option is to take her to Africa and spread her ashes. *Out of Africa* is her favorite movie, and at a time when my parents acted as a married couple, my dad took her on a dream hunting safari to South Africa for two weeks in Namibia. Here. This is a photo album from their trip. She could not stop talking about her time there and how we needed to go together."

Emelia carefully flips through the pages, explaining what they were doing, the people her parents met, the animals they hunted. I was in awe as her mum looked so happy in those photos. This did enlighten me that Emelia gets her olive skin and dark features from her father, but I see the slight resemblance of her mum in her face. As she places it back, I finally take in that the tables on both sides of the bed are not nightstands, but actual mini bookcases. Looking to the left one closest to me, I notice it is slap full of books as well, but must be of her favorites because they look very worn and older. I notice a few of the authors like Dante, Poe, and Bronte along with lots of worn paperbacks. Leaning over to see her bend down to the one closest to her, I find it is filled with photo albums and a small jewelry box. After a few more memory lane trips, we had lunch, and with several things on my docket I needed to work through with Kent, I headed out for the day. Though completely exhausted from our escapades, I took a run first, and now I am back at my Airbnb to check in with Kent.

"How's it going man?" I ask when I enter the house.

"Going well. Just catching up on emails and booking a few more photo shoots for you. You are a hot commodity, and we need to capitalize on it." He looks up at me with a concerned face. "Your lady friend going to be okay with all that?"

"Yes. She knows I modeled for Calvin Klein and that I do photoshoots for magazines and sponsors. Maybe try to leave the other women out as much as possible though." I get the look that tells me I am trailing a fine line between trying to have a girlfriend and remain the sex symbol several of my sponsors want me to be, so I throw my hands up. "I know man, I get it. Whatever needs to be done," I gripe as I walk off to my room to shower.

Chapter 18: Don't Make It Awkward

I won't lie, a few days later and I still feel like I am walking awkwardly with the soreness between my legs, but I'm at work. The bridge ladies making their appearance noticed as they catch up on Lucas's gossip like my library is now the mingling cafe for them. No lie, they have taken over the sitting area, drinking their morning tea or coffee, and someone brings in pastries every morning. Knowing Lucas will make an appearance at some point on his way to the gym or physical therapy. They swoon over him, and us together.

Already wedding planning, and Lucas becoming a staple in the community. I laugh and push off their suggestions, but Lucas always has the look of processing it all and appeasing them. Which makes me want to coward behind my wall, because in reality, how will this work long term? Oliver runs in, breaking my thoughts up.

"Lucas, I am ready for our workout this morning." This kid has so much excitement, you would think it is Christmas morning.

"Alright, well let's get going then." I see them both off as they race to Lucas's hot red, now I know a McLaren Artura. They take off down the road, and I see Oliver's mom and dad walk up.

"Good morning, Masons. Thanks for letting Oliver hang with Lucas. They have a good time together."

"They really do," his mom speaks up. "How are you doing, dear?"

"I am doing pretty well. Thanks for asking. Just enjoying the summer and Lucas being around."

"Oliver is too. Do you know how long Lucas has left here?"

"The first race is on the weekend of June 17th, but we really haven't talked about what is to come after that, as I know the schedule goes through October. Not sure what his plan is for the remainder of the season and after. I guess it is the elephant in the room that we keep ignoring."

"I get that," his dad speaks up. "Well just let us know, hon. We would like to prepare Oliver before he disappears." His wife slaps him hard in the chest.

"Not disappear, honey. He did not mean it that way. Just his schedule for when he is not around."

"No, of course. That makes sense," I say as I give a sheepish grin. "Please excuse me, I am going to get back to work. It was nice talking to you." Quickly walking back into the library, I take a deep breath and turn the opposite direction from the bridge club ladies and head straight to my book cart to start reshelving. *What the hell!* We are three weeks into this thing we have going on, and as much as I am just trying to enjoy the *now*, my heart is already crying in his absence. My head is torn whether to walk away from this before it becomes any more or just go along with the craziest ride of my life, knowing I will be the wreckage in the end.

"Hey, Marcy, are you good handling story time today at noon?"

"Of course. Do whatever you need to do."

"Thanks, I have something I need to take care of. Just call me if you need me." I grab my stuff and head out. I head to the place where I am typically not ever found. Right now, I need space and quiet. Right now, I need to figure out how much I can handle, if I can handle any of it if he breaks my heart. Because right now, I feel like this should have never happened to begin with knowing how breakable I am. Why did he keep pushing me? Sure, I wanted him, sure I enjoy his company, but I told him I would try. Maybe this is me done trying now.

Jumping on my bike, I head down over and down to the lighthouse. The lighthouse sits up higher and is surrounded by rock walls that include many large boulders. One particular at the point of all off to the right a bit. The area is marked off to the public, due to some reconstruction happening. Only the lighthouse owner, workers, and the marine conservationists can break through the rope. For me, Benny is a family friend and allows me to come and go as I please. As this is a place where I would frequent when I was younger just as much as I have frequented in my adult years. I arrive at my spot, being thankful the breeze and water is calm today as I take my seat out on the boulder on the edge.

Pulling my phone out the pocket of my shorts, I am hit with a dozen or more missed calls from Lucas, Marcy, and Mrs. Baxter. Along with several text messages from Lucas. Scrolling through he is panicking and at my house with Winston.

I send back a text letting him know I am okay and will be home in a couple of hours or so. As well as checking in with Marcy, only for her to tell me Lucas is pissed and frantic about me dropping off the radar. Letting her know I am fine, I put my phone on silent and lay back on the rock, with my arms splayed out.

"Take me now!" I shout to the sky. Then I just lay there for hours. Not thinking, not talking, just listening to the waves hit the rocks and water spraying itself on the island. It is a serene sound. One I could easily listen to forever without another care in the world. Unfortunately, I do have other cares in the world. One is Winston. Two, the library. Three, the people of this town look to me to make things happen. Four, well four now is Lucas. Lucas *fucking* Stratton. I was fine before he was pushed into my life, and I need to make sure I am fine when he is gone. Everyone leaves me. This is not a trust issue or even a me issue. It is a fact.

Lucas's POV

It is bloody six in the evening when I hear her front door open and spot her walking in. My first instinct is to rush to her, check her over to make sure she is fine, but my anger gets the best of me before I can show I even care.

"Where the bloody hell have you been all damn day!" I shout, stunning her. She leaves me surprised when I see her face shift as her wall goes back up.

"What's it to you anyway? I needed time to think so I did. I have not and will not answer to anyone. Especially someone who is not in my future."

"What the fuck you mean not in your future?"

"Just that. I am not keeping you from your dream, your career. You will be leaving in a month. Then starts your track-to-track racing across the states. Then after, you will be heading back to Europe, right? So allow me to address the big ass elephant in the room. US! You, not staying."

Running my hand down my face in frustration, I glare at her.

"What happened to you today? Where the hell is this coming from? Did Kent call you?" I am running through everything in my head of what could have changed since I saw her at nine this morning to her disappearing act by noon.

"Just chatter. Chatter about your plans that I know nothing about. And why the hell would Kent call me? What are you not telling me?"

"You infuriate me woman!" Throwing my hands up, I try not to punch a wall. "Traitor," I grunt to Winston with a side eye as he is now crouched down beside her.

"Let me get this straight. You somehow got in your head today that I was just leaving you. Without discussing with me, you make the decision to end this. End this right now. Without even considering my plans, my feelings, my wants. That becoming a royal bitch in front of me, would push me to walk away?" She shifts her eyes, so they are now looking everywhere but me. "Get it through your thick skull darling, I see you. I see you like no one else does. I know you because I know your heart. I have your heart… Has any other man ever given you what I have? Loved you like I have? Made you scream and orgasm like I have? Make you have tingling senses when they are near?" Her wet depleted gaze meets mine as she shakes her head no. "Christ Emelia. Yes, I love you, because I do not know how else to explain what the hell I am feeling and what this is. I would bleed for you; I ache for you. That time I called you in the middle of night, was not just to check in like I forgot. It was because I woke up with a jolt as if my subconscious knew something was not right with you. That something was wrong. The same feeling I had today before I even left the gym. I brushed it off, thinking that cannot happen twice. To only get back to the library to find you gone, fucking gone, with no one knowing where the hell you were." I hastily walk over to her as her face is now buried in her hands, crying. "Please do not cry, darling. I do not mean to make you gutted, but you need to understand I am here. Racing may be my career, but you are now my dream." She collapses against me, shaking in a fit of disarray. I carry her to the couch holding her as tight as I can, while she gives in, laying her head on my shoulder.

"I am so sorry," she squeaks out.

"I do not want your regretful apologies, Emelia. Just your love and trust. I need this, we need this before we can move forward."

Looking up at me, tears glimmer in her eyes. "You have it, Lucas. You have my all, and that is why I am so scared and the unknown hurts so bad."

"Damn, I love you, and I am trying to understand you. Promise me you will never go rogue again without us having a conversation first." She nods her head. "I need to hear you say it, Emelia. Say it out loud."

"I promise, Lucas. We will talk first." She cuddles back into my chest and arms as her breathing finally begins to calm. All I can do is run my fingers through her hair and be thankful she is safely back home in my arms.

"I must learn to be content with being happier than I deserve." — Jane Austen, Pride and Prejudice

Chapter 19: Everything Will Change

Another emotional headache this morning, except I am being held down in bed by Lucas's arm and leg sprawled on top of me. With Winston to my left and nowhere to move, I start to sweat and slightly panic. Panic setting in as every inch I free myself, I am pressed more into the mattress or Winston moves closer. For the love of all things holy…

"Let me out of here," I huff under my breath. Pulling out of the covers from the top and not so gracefully rolling over Winston to the floor, I look back over the bed to see my two guys roll into each and snuggle. Shaking my head, I quietly sniggle as I make my escape out of the bedroom. Heading across the living, I look out the large bay window and see white caps of the rolling waves and cloudy skies. *Peachy,* looks like a rainy Friday. I am thankful that I slept through the night because my nerves have been shot lately. Though I have been keeping track. My sleep pattern and dreams are less intense when Lucas stays over.

Jesus! What am I doing? I think to myself, as I make my English tea. Lucas is right, I need to quit being such a bitch, trying to push him away every chance I feel insecure. He is handling my tortured past as best he can. I really have not been fair to him or us for that matter. To be fair, we are three weeks into this relationship that seemed to have started as soon as we met. How the hell am I supposed to get my mind wrapped around all this and not have insecurities? He must have his own apprehensions but is way better about keeping them hidden. Speaking of hidden, what did he mean about Kent calling me? There must be something going on that Lucas has not disclosed to me.

Turning around to grab my teacup to add honey, I hear the bedroom door open. Winston comes padding out and heads straight for the doggie door to the outside. Following behind him is a tousled mess of a sexy Lucas. Even on his worst days, he looks like an amazing piece of art. One you can't pull your eyes away because you know there is so much more to the beautiful story in front of you.

"Good morning," I ease out with a smile, trying to gauge his mood. I remember all of last evening, and this man has a temper. Not one that would physically hurt me, but to be able to fill up the whole room with tension and fury. A seriously demanding presence that I was not expecting when I walked in my house. Again, three weeks in, I barely know him, but my heart and soul is already his. Everyone has a flaw, and I am pinning his overbearing anger issues are his.

"Darling," he addresses me while looking out of the bay window himself before making his way over to me in the kitchen. He plants a quick kiss on my temple. "Are you hungry?" he asks.

"I could eat."

"French omelets sound good?"

"Perfect," I say back, taking my seat at the kitchen bar.

He begins cutting vegetables, breaking eggs, and mixing. I sit there quietly watching him not wanting to start an argument but have questions to ask.

"Just ask, Emelia. I feel your inquiring eyes and nervous vibes."

"You asked if Kent called me and seemed concerned about it. Why?"

Putting his hands on the counter, he sighs in frustration. I watch him as he gathers his thoughts, the shift in his stance as his jaw tenses.

"Well, we got some news last weekend while we were testing." Taking a deep breath, I wait for him to continue.

"Team owner wants me back on the track for the British GT3 series as well as the American GT4 series for the remainder of the season. That means two races a month and lots of traveling. On top of having to be in the track area the whole week for testing, sponsor photo shoots, and meetings. Plus, CK will be a large sponsor for the American series and has asked me to be the face." He pauses, assessing me from the side of the counter, before turning around to pour his mixture into the pan.

"Wow, that all sounds incredible. I am thinking not many drivers are asked to do both series let alone one for the whole season? I have seen your previous CK ads, so I am assuming they are more underwear ads."

He nods his head, keeping his eyes on the pan, as he pushes the omelet mix around, preparing to flip with the spatula. After he flips and folds it, he places it on a plate and begins the next one. We are both quiet, and though my mind is swirling with all this new information, I need him to make the first move. I need him to discuss his plans with me on how this is going to work and be stable for us. I am insecure, jealous, and have a track record of everyone leaving me, so he knows this can't be good. Hence why it has taken him till now to tell me.

Lucas's POV

Shit! Fuck! Bloody fucking hell! After yesterday, the last thing I want to do is have her thoughts become realizations. The truth is, these facts change everything. No longer will I be here three weeks out of the month through October as I planned. I will be lucky to be here even for two weeks, and some of those weeks will be back-to-back at tracks. Stateside and across the pond. Ideally, I would love for her to be with me all the time, but that is not realistic. She has a life here; one I will not ask her to give up for me. Plus, race weeks are grueling and stressful, my temper gets the best of me during the rough times, and according to my past, I party like an animal to relieve stress regardless of how things are going. This is going to be a fucking shit show, but I need to convince her otherwise. Because the thought of losing her right now or down the road is driving me crazy.

Placing a plate in front of her, I take a seat next to her.

"Darling, this does not change anything." Her mouth agape looking in shock tells me I need to be more cautious in approaching this with her.

"It changes my time here, and our time spent together the next several months, but not the fact that I want to be with you. I will be here every moment I can, and I would also really love it if you could travel with me some, or fly out the weekends of the races. I know that is not possible for all, but we can look at the schedule to see which ones would be fitting for you." She is slowly chewing her omelet, not looking at me. Her body is slouched which throws signals of defeat and unwillingness.

"Don't you start, darling. We are going to make it through this. We are meant to be together, and I will be damned in hell if you think otherwise. Trust me, Emelia, I need you to trust me on the plans I will make for us, on our time apart. Trust that I love you enough to always come back." Reaching over, I pull her chin toward me, making her face me. Her golden sun eyes have turned into an after fire amber glow. Running the pads of my fingers down the side of her face, she leans into them. "Trust me," I whisper. Lingering moments go by, before I get a yes under her breath, so I take it.

Not wanting to push anymore, I take this small win and acceptance, knowing balancing the two most important things in my life will be the most difficult thing I have had to do up to this point. Emelia was completely unplanned. Meeting a woman like her, falling in love was never the plan. Never been in any plan I have had for myself, the chances of me bloody screwing this up is very very high.

Chapter 20: Whatever It Takes

Over a week in, post the breaking news, and we have fallen back into our previous routine, and Lucas has basically moved in. Knowing the weeks we have left together are drifting away as quick as a message in a bottle being pulled away by the current. We decided to do whatever it takes for us to come out at the end of these next few months together, and then we will deal with the next obstacles. Knowing if our relationship can take all the hits and lashes that are to come, there is hope for us.

I have been at the library all week, as Marcy is covering Friday and Saturday for me since I will be out in Virginia with Lucas. It has been a long time since I have flown, so my nerves are already amped up over that. The other half is being thrown into Lucas's world and being out of my bubble. Excitement and uneasiness fill my mind as I try to finish up tasks to get ready for next week's events. We start Blues on the Beach tonight and movie night on Friday, and as of right now, my checklist is complete–three times over. It is just a matter of vendors and people showing up to fulfill commitments made. Hopefully all goes well tonight and will just flow like that for the remainder of the week.

Lucas has been busy with Kent, doing online interviews, gym, as well as finishing up physical therapy. He has really been pushing himself this week to be ready for the first race in a few weeks, along with using his racing simulator to learn the rest of the American tracks. I can also see the excitement he has about being Europe-bound. He tries his best to conceal it when he is around me, but I have been listening to the interviews and podcasts all week to know better. Racing is not only his career, but also part of what makes him breathe, tick, and he loves it so much. Any chance he has to get behind the wheel of a race car, is a chance he will never deny himself, nor do I ever expect him to. Neither of us saw this coming, and we both have our lives on opposite sides of the world. Fate might have brought us together again, but I also know fate and happy endings are not my biggest fans, so I am having to keep my reality checks regularly to be grounded. Lucas makes it easy to dream up future plans and go with the flow.

It is six in the evening as Marcy and I scramble to replace a last minute food truck that was canceled due to an illness, and the band ended up on the other end near the seaside Merry-Go-round. So we are already an hour behind as they make their way over to us, and we still have a sound check to complete. The townees and vacationers have already started making their way down to the beach to find spots to set beach chairs and towels out. At this point, I am typically able to welcome the guests and watch in awe as I watch creatures of habit set up in the same place every single time, the newbies not realizing said spots are already taken, but always politely shown another place they can set up. Then you have late comers who try to squeeze in wherever they can, but after the ruckus they cause once arrived, typically are the first to head out.

By the time the band is ready and looks like most of everyone has grabbed food, drinks, and look to be settled, it is eight o'clock. We made up for some time, but a forty-five-minute delay with a band that is notorious for an encore, is going to make for a long night. Not having heard from Lucas since this morning, I sent over a text letting him know I have a spot up on one of the sand dunes, looking over the crowd, but it also has a pretty clear view of the stage and away from all the ruckus. Once the show starts, I finally head over to the Shuckin' Truck, grabbing some lobster rolls, lobster grilled bites, bacon wrapped scallops, and of course a pail of oysters with a couple of beers. By the time I make it back to our area, I see Lucas there sitting in one of the chairs I set up while on his phone, with Winston laying by his side.

"Hey, stranger," I say as I get closer. "How did you find your way up here?"

"Oh, I am happy to see you," he says as he stands up to help me with the bags of food and kisses me on the cheek.

"Marcy showed me the way. She said this is always your spot."

I smile. "It is. Hope you enjoy the view as much as I do." Bending down, I give Winston an ear rub.

"This is the perfect view from where I am." Looking back up at him, I catch his imploring gaze back down to me. All I can do is blush, while tossing him a plate and beer from my bag, as I can get the rest of the food laid out on the little table I put out in front of us.

The rest of the evening is spent chowing down on good food, throwing back some beers, and enjoying each other's presence under the stars and stage lights while the rock reggae band plays into the night. At some point, the ocean picks up a bit causing a cooler breeze to blow through. Lucas surprises me with a blanket that he wraps me in before placing me in his lap to hold. Listening to the rhythm of his heartbeat, it seems to overcome the music and ocean waves and take over my hearing. *Lup-dup, lup-dup, lup-dup, lup-dup,* consistently until I feel him wiggle underneath me, and then I hear a sudden skip, hitch in breath causing the beating to be a little faster until it goes back down to the calm and slow *lup-dup* that pulls me into a relaxed sleep.

Lucas's POV

The last interview ran over this afternoon, as it was for a European podcast for the GT series. We were making the announcement with the McLaren team owners of my return, and what is happening for the rest of the season. I was warned by Kent before the schedule of interviews started this week, I am not to mention having a girlfriend, as we have a few more sponsor contracts to sign, and we all know, single chap and sex sells is better than "off the market chap." We tried to dodge those questions best we could, knowing Kent has already put measures on keeping Emelia being at the V.I.R with us as secret as possible. Something tells me keeping her under the radar is going to be hard to do. She is a unique beauty that draws others in. Whether she wants to or not. Her smile lights up a room because it is so rare to even those closest to her, and her true personality is something that must be earned, but she treats everyone as a friend.

All of that gets pushed to the back of mind as I sit here with her nestled in my embrace against my body. She takes all stress and worry away from my mind when she is near. Not just because I know she has personally been to hell and back within her own life, so I feel anything I undergo is not even in comparison, but because she is my calm. Kissing the top of her head, I wrap her up in a blanket as she sleeps on top of me in the chair, and I take in the music and waves surrounding us. Hoping all goes well this weekend with the car, with the crew, and Emelia. We already made plans for Winston to join her on the flight and be with her, as if anything, she will be more comfortable with him around. With Kent and I flying out early in the morning for meetings and a few modeling sessions in the late afternoon with CK, I am already looking forward to seeing Emelia on Friday at the track. Since my attention has to be there, he has made arrangements for her and Winston to be chauffeured over and shown around until I get a break at noon. He has also already warned Emelia and I to have as little PDA in public as possible, because there are always cameras everywhere. People can gossip, but without proof, their words mean nothing. Emelia is trying to take it all in and understand where he is coming from in terms of my sponsors and deals, and in time, we will be able to announce "us," but I also know this is for the best for her in order to keep her out of the spotlight. Protect her from the world of tabloids and gossip. Protect her from the evil people that will say anything to hurt someone, and even all the jealous women that will make a run at her. The longer I can keep her to myself, the better we will fare at the end of this racing season.

"There was nothing special with the way he looked at her but her heart raced even with a glance." — Pushpa Rana, Just the Way I Feel

Chapter 21: Game On

"Hey, Bec. Winston and I made it to the state for lovers. What are you doing that you are not answering your phone right now? Call me back when you get this. I have to go find our driver and head to the track. Love you. Bye." Winston and I take the elevator down, because carrying the big bear down the escalator is not going to happen. As soon as we step out, I luckily see our names on the sign a tall guy in a black suit and hat is holding. We walk over and I introduce ourselves, and he lets me know his name is Rick and that he will be chauffeuring us around for the whole weekend. Wherever we want to go, no matter what time of day. Helping me with my carry-on, Winston and I follow him out of the airport to a sleek black Cadillac sedan. Even then inside is leather and suede mixed, and I am actually nervous about Winston getting the car. Rick senses my hesitation and pulls a blanket out of the trunk and lays down on the back seat for Winston to lay on. Once we are all settled, we are on our way to the track, or *the VIR*. It takes us almost two hours to reach the track from the airport as I find this place is in the middle of nowhere, but ginormous.

Lucas had let me know prior we would be staying at The Lodge for the weekend that I see off to my left. Looks very cozy. For the actual race weekend, since he will be here all week, we would be staying in The Villas at South Bend, which I have to think is on the other side of this massive track. I can only see one corner of this track, but I can hear several cars out there.

"Miss, I just called Mr. Lawson and let him know you are here. He is on his way to get you," Rick states.

"Thank you, Rick."

I soon see Kent coming around the corner, so Winston and I make our way toward him.

"How was the flight?" he asks as he gives me a hug and pets Winston.

"It was great, and Rick was great, so thank you."

"My pleasure. Lucas would not have it any other way but the best for you." I gesture a smile. "Please follow me. Lucas is still out testing but should be coming back in here in about twenty minutes or so. I will warn you, the car has been shit all day, so he has not been in the best mood. Fingers crossed this time out showed improvements."

"Oh, really? I am happy to just sit back until things calm down. I definitely do not want to get in the way of anything or be a distraction."

"Are you kidding me? You may be the welcomed distraction he needs right now and take the heat off the crew," he states as he laughs and continues walking on, while Winston and I try to keep up. He leads us up to the stands and points out the car Lucas is in, so I know what I am looking for. Before I know it, Lucas comes zooming by in his McLaren race car, followed by a few cars that look almost the same as his, leaving my heart racing. I have never before been around such a fast and loud environment. My eyes follow the cars as they zip through a few turns, disappear into another part of the track I am unable to see from my view, only to show up on the side flying through the straight part, around another corner and past me again. This happens for another six times before Kent lets me know they are pulling into the pits. Also telling me to stay put, and he will send Lucas over as soon as he can.

Thirty minutes go by before I see Lucas from a distance heading over. I can tell he is trying to be casual and not completely just jolt over here. We have already gotten an earful from Kent on how we are to behave in public this weekend, including at the track, most importantly. We are to save all PDA for behind closed doors. I have to say though, Winston did not get the same memo we did, because he wiggled out of my grip and took off to Lucas as fast as he could. Practically jumping into his arms as Lucas brings him back over.

"Hey, you," he says with a large grin.

"Hey yourself, Mister Cool."

"Mister Cool, huh?" he asks as he leans over the fence in front of the stands, looking up at me.

"Uh, yah. Who else do I know that drives a cool ass car at high speeds around a curvy track at the VIR?" I giggle.

"I want to kiss that cute little mouth of yours so bad right now. I am also not sure if I want to correct your race lingo or not yet," he wheezes as he double overs with his own laughs.

"All I can do is try. This is completely foreign to me."

"I know. Just cute is all because you are trying. But first, let me correct you on just one thing." I slant my eyes at him inquisitively. "It is not the VIR, but V.I.R." My mouth forms in the shape of a ring, and he gives me the sexiest grin. Clapping his hands together, he says, "So let me run you over to meet the crew, and then I have a surprise for you back over at the lodge, while I finish up here for the day."

"Okay, lead the way, Mister Cool."

He is quick to grab my hand to lead me down the steps and gives it a tight squeeze before letting go. Running his hands through his sweaty tousled hair, he says, "This is going to be so hard not touching you, while you are so close."

"Just think of the things you get to do to me once we are in our room to make up for it," I state, giving him a wink. I hear a slight chuckle out of him while he shakes his head, leading the way.

Before I know it, I am in a large garage area where twenty plus people are running around and staring at computers. He introduces me to everyone as his sister's friend–*which I was not keen on but was prepped prior on*– and wanted to check out the track and team for an article I am writing. *Gosh, I hate lying to people like this.* He slowly introduces me to everyone, and I learn the older bald gentleman Henry is his crew chief, the six-four suave Italian, Lorenzo is Lucas's right hand man when it comes to all the technology and computer work needed on the car. He is the one that goes through the mock trials with him and can click a few buttons that changes I believe the amount of horsepower and adjustments in the car. I literally just keep nodding as they spew out their lingo to each other like I have a clue what they are saying.

Soon we make our way around to several others, and I am impressed to see that Lucas has five women working as part of his pit crew. Two I notice are watching the screens that look to be his laps ran along with a few others. One is up under the car tweaking something before rolling out, as I see two more women help push the car out of the garage and prep for Lucas to jump back in. I take a mental note to mention my awe-shocked impress-ness to him later.

"Hey, Kent, After Emelia watches a few runs, can you take her over to the lodge?"

"Sure. Because right after this run, you have three more press interviews with the team, and then you are done for the day."

"Thanks, man," he states as he pats Kent on the back. I see him nod to someone behind me, and before I know it, I have one of the women next to me handing me a headset.

"Hey, I am Kate. Come over here so you can watch with Ariene and I and listen in."

"Thanks. This is crazy exciting," I mention as Winston and I follow her over to the tv booth and stools. Winston takes a quick flop down to the ground, sensing we are going to be here for a bit.

Ariene and Kate are great. As I watch one screen with his in-car camera on and another from giving me an outside view, they walk me through each turn he takes, when he is breaking, giving the car more gas. Going over his driving style, like Lucas loves to wait until the last minute to start breaking which they say most of the time works in his favor, but there are times it has not. Especially when he is stuck in lap traffic, and everyone is slamming on their brakes. He takes turns as tight as he can to not allow any room for another car to catch up. I begin staring at the in-camera shot, his hands are calm, and he moves the wheel like fluid. There are no jerky motions as he literally at one-point hits 186mph on a straightaway, and I am left dumbfounded by the grace this man carries driving a car that fast, and he makes it seem like it never phases him.

After two more laps, Kent comes and gets me to take me back to the lodge. I turn back around, handing my headset back to Kate who leans in close to me.

"Just so you know, we know that you are not a sister's friend."

"What makes you say that?" I ask, trying to keep my poker face.

"Woman's intuition, I guess. Besides, Lucas has never brought a woman into a garage let alone his own sisters. We will keep it a secret because the men are too clueless. We are rooting for you girl because you must mean something special to him."

"Well, thank you. I appreciate the silence on it and knowing I have you ladies in my corner. I think it is pretty badass of you to be immersed in this world."

Kate gives me a fist pump that I shyly return before Kent leads Winston and I out of the garage and to a golf cart that takes us back to the lodge.

Lucas's POV

"Man, that was the best and fastest lap of the day. You showing off for someone?" Lorenzo shouts through my headset. All I can do is chuckle.

"No, Lo, just out here doing my job."

"Sure man," he says as he chuckles to himself. I pull into the pits, and as I bring my car to a stop, I glance into the garage to see that Emelia must have already left.

"Don't worry, man, she saw your awesome lap!" Henry shouts over to me as I pull my gloves and helmet off. "Kent just took her over in the golf cart."

Trying to play it off, I say, "O that's cool… Come on, let's get me out of this gear and move on to the next thing. Henry, I would not touch a thing on the car. She drives like a dream, just where we want her."

He gives me a quick thumbs up as he takes a call. Once I shower and dress in my jeans and race team shirt, I see Kent whip around the corner.

"Ready, speed racer?"

"Sure, let's go."

Once on the golf cart to the interview tent, he lets me know my girl is all checked in and getting settled. Even letting me know I need to get my head right, and not fight anyone, because there are plenty of guys around partaking in glances, and even a few brave ones that are approaching.

"Really, man? That is what you need to tell me before I must interview?" I grumble, but he gives me that look to check my shit. I pause.

"Got it, my shit's checked!" But in my head, I am thinking that I will hurt a bloody bloke that tries anything with her. Also it has me re-thinking that as much as I want her with me, until we are announced, it might not be the best thing to have her be around so much testosterone when I cannot be next to her all the time. I must focus out there on the track, absolutely no room for error.

Kent pulls up next to the tent, and with one look to each other, game face sets in. Knowing I need to be extra with my game, as I see Mario, my European teammate on an enlarged screen next to where I will be sitting. His smug face is already in position to strike.

Game on, you barmy tosser.

chapter 22: Start Your Engine

Being in shock is an understatement after I walk into the bar of the lodge and see my best friend Becca sitting in a chair waiting for me. So much gleeful screaming just happened, everyone is staring at us thinking we lost our minds. Bec is quick to let everyone know I am her long lost lover, and we are re-kindling after seven years apart. Only to be rewarded with applause, causing my whole body to heat up with embarrassment because attention is the last thing I want.

"You look good, E. You really do," Bec says as we hug one more time before sitting across from each other in the lounge area.

"Thanks, Bec. I feel good; I feel relaxed right now. But still cannot believe you are here with me. How did this even happen?"

"Well, your lover boy got my number and called me last week and asked if he arranged everything, could I come out. How could I turn down seeing you a few weeks early with you only a few hours away? I see he is trying to get on my good side, and right now, he is doing a damn good job," she says followed by a laugh that I have missed so much in person. Hearing it is one thing but seeing it is even better. Bec's whole face lights up, and her eyes sparkle and bounce around when her face moves while she is laughing, along with it draws in the attention of everyone in the best way. Because you just want to know what made this beautiful woman laugh so hard but be so poised at the same time. Laughing with her, I say, "He is a good one, but I won't lie and say I am not waiting for his pitchfork and horns to show."

"Still believing he is the devil in disguise?"

"No, yes, no, ugh… I don't know. He is just too good, especially with someone like me."

"E, you are sooo good. Maybe he is what you need to show you how good *you* really are. You have been dealt some shitty cards, my friend, but that does not mean any of it defines you in the end. Now enough heavy talk, cause you have me here for a few more hours, before lover boy comes and steals you away from me."

"Are Emily and Pharm-boy back at the house?" She giggles at the nickname I call her husband because she knows how I pride myself on the cleverness of it.

"Yes. They are having a daddy daughter day at the zoo. But hey, you get the whole family in a few weeks for the Fourth. I cannot wait to get back home and see your face every day. Along with all the festivities."

"Me either. For me, it is not officially summer until you are there and stirring up the town."
We both laugh and take a sip of our drinks. She goes about telling me about her trip up here, and we catch up from the busy week and plan for when she and the family are back home, along with how many nights she will be sleeping over with me since her parents will be spoiling Emily, and Brian will be trying to catch up on sleep and be lazy. When it seems barely any time has gone by at all, Lucas shows up. Quickly letting us know we have been in the same spot for several hours that included many drinks served.

"Oh, lover boy. You just could not stay away a bit longer, could you?" she spits out with a grin.

"Honestly, no I couldn't. I have been sitting over there for the last hour with some of the guys, while watching my girl let loose. I will say you bring out a different side of her I was not expecting."

"And that my new friend is how it will remain. Ho's before bro's!" Bec shouts while we give each other a high five, and Lucas doesn't even know what to say.

"Okay, my new found friend, am I able to take this beautiful woman away with me now?"

"As long as you do not break her, you may. And I mean that with my full heart, lover boy. She is my person, and I would do anything for her. Including hiding a body." I am too busy sniggling at these two banter that I almost miss the blood drain from Lucas's face. Bec may be tipsy and loud,

but he already knows she means what she says when it comes
to me.

I get up and throw myself into Bec's arms as we hug
and whisper in each other's ears and laugh.

"Okay you two, time to break it up. Becca's ride is
here. And it seems I might need to sober you up before
dinner."

"Who me?" I say innocently while hanging onto
Bec's arm.

"Come on, we will walk her out." Lucas leads as Bec
and I remain in linked arms following behind. Only for her to
comment on his nice ass, and my loud whisper of agreement
that he hears and turns back to me, giving me a wink.
Still without touching, we watch my best friend ride away.
He leans over a little and says, "I am going to walk over to
the bar to have another drink, while you head up to our room.
I will have Rick," he nods to the side of me, and Rick
magically appears, "walk you up safely. I will be up there in
twenty minutes or less."

"Okay, Mister Cool." I turn around giggling and
follow Rick and Winston to the elevator.

Lucas's POV

I am still standing in the spot where I watched Emelia
walk away to our room. She has me so infatuated with her to
the point I am annoyed with myself. In such a jiffy, she has
become everything I never knew I needed or even wanted.
Then seeing that vivacious personality come to life as I
watched from afar, only solidifies my feelings, but a
reminder I have a way to go to earn that place with her.
Becca is home to her, and I want to be that for her also. I only
get little fire starters of that side of her, but she put on a full
display with Becca tonight for the whole place to see. I had to
keep the guys from going over there and bothering them. One
married and one taken, not a great combination when it

comes to other men hitting on other men's women. Not because I do not think either one of them could handle themselves because I am sure as shit both of them could make any grown man cry at the rate they were going tonight, but because I personally could not watch that happen. Emelia is mine and only mine, and Becca is her married best friend, so I have a responsibility to her as well.

Walking back over to the table, I hear the guys still talking about those two fine pieces of ass in the lounge tonight.

Pep is the first to speak up as I approach. "Hey man, so when are you going to introduce us to your sister's friend and other friend?"

Trying not to look too annoyed, I shake my head at his words. "Bollock's man, quit being such a wanker. I introduced you all to Emelia this afternoon in the garage, and her friend has already left for the evening. Besides I hear they both are married."

"Seriously? Well that ruins my plans for the evening." Lorenzo spouts.

"What in hell plans did you have?" I grimace at my tone, trying to not look as if I want to strangle this man in front of me.

"I was going to ask her to dinner and swoon her with the Lo charm."

"You're serious right now? It is best you all use your judgment and leave that poor girl alone. She is too good for all of us, so no chance in hell she would date anyone in the race world."

"Well for a "married" lady, the way she was eyeing you out earlier seems like one man at this table might have a shot."

"Shut up, Pep. It definitely is not you." Throwing back my beer, I slam the empty glass on the table. "I will see you boilers in the early morning. Night." I stride off with them giving me hell about ditching them early tonight. *Sorry boys, my best kept secret is waiting in my room for me.*

I walk into the room to see Emelia passed out in bed, but in the most sexist checkered flag outfit I have ever seen. Next to her is a racing book for dummies. I quickly snap a picture of this impeccably adorable sexy view with my phone before deciding to wake her. Gently nudging her on her side, she rolls over and says, "Gentlemen, start your engines" in a mumbled whisper.

Whispering in her ear, I say, "Believe me, darling, my engine has started." as I bite and suck her ear, luring her awake. She lets out a soft whimper that makes me want to come undone at this very moment. I run my hand softly up and down her body as she continues to make small moans, but when her eyes start to flutter open, she has the biggest grin on her face that makes me laugh.

"How you feeling there, darling?"

"Oh just fine now that you are here, Mister Cool." She starts to giggle at her own joke. "Please, don't stop doing what you were doing."

"Baby, I am just getting started with you. But I do have a question."

"Ask a way."

"What were you planning on doing with this little number?" I ask as I pop the pleather of her booty shorts against her upper thigh.

"Oh, this little old thing? Just trying it out to see if I could pull it off tomorrow at the garage so maybe I could blend in a little more," she says at a deadpan.

"Bollocks, Emelia, you cannot wear this outside of this room and with no one other than me." I growl, and as I feel my temper rise, she starts laughing.

"You are so silly, sir. Do you really think someone like me would waltz around like this? TSK TSK, you must not know me at all."

Before she can even move from the bed, I have her arms pinned above her head in my hands, as I hover over her body.

"Oh, I know you very well, darling, and I also know you evidently want to play games tonight." Bending down to her ear, I whisper, "Let us play, how long can Emelia go without me inside her."
The look of worry lights up her amber eyes. "You wouldn't!"
And as quickly as those words escape her mouth, my shirt is off, and I am tying it around her wrists then securing her arms over the middle of the headboard where there is just enough of a point to give a hook.

"Don't worry baby, I dreamt of doing this to you last night while I was alone." I walk into the closest and come back with two of my ties. Slowly and gently tying each ankle to the best posts, allowing her legs to spread apart, I am again taken back by her beauty. Her eyes are glowing with desire as the light bounces off her freckles.

"How much do you love this outfit?"

"Why? I just bought it. Wait…are you going to cut it off?"

"I will get you a new one," I say as I rip down the center, exposing her bare chest and tug it down off her bottom then ripping the sides, finally freeing her from it.

"Now it is playtime, and I think I will start down here." I lay light kisses up and down her thighs to her center. She is already squirming, and I make note this is going to be an incredibly fun night for the both of us.

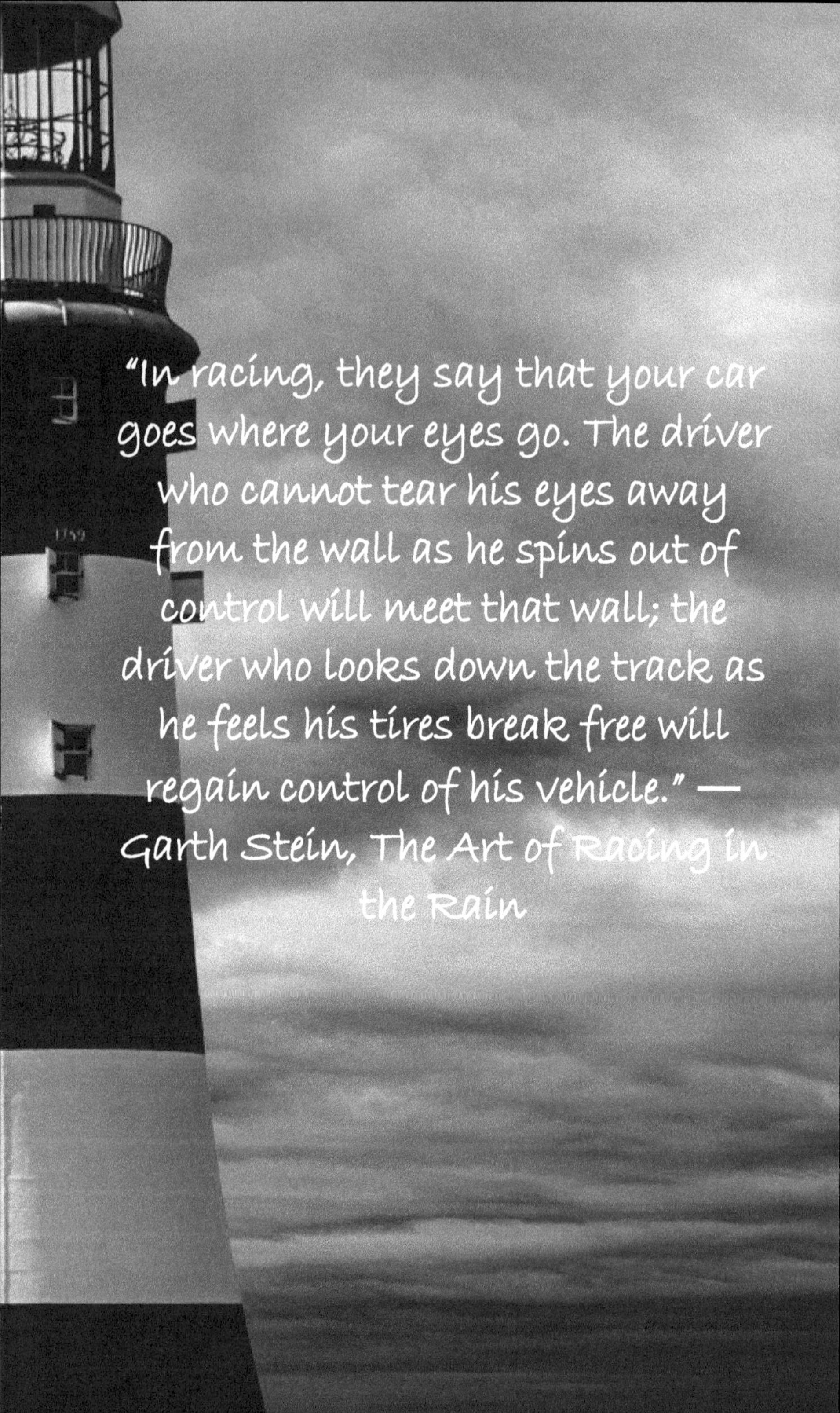

"In racing, they say that your car goes where your eyes go. The driver who cannot tear his eyes away from the wall as he spins out of control will meet that wall; the driver who looks down the track as he feels his tires break free will regain control of his vehicle." — Garth Stein, The Art of Racing in the Rain

Chapter 23: Rapid Fire

It is six AM, and I am still lying in bed, naked and completely sore from last night's activities. Lucas, on the other hand, still found enough energy to get up at five to go for his run with Winston before his team meeting at seven this morning. Me on the other hand, I am still contemplating how I am going to function today with barely any sleep and a sore body that will have me waddling like a penguin again.
 Knock. Knock.
Surely he did not forget his key, I think to myself as I slowly roll out of the bed, wrapping myself up in the bedsheet.
Knock. Knock. Knock.

"Hold your horses, I'm coming," I grumble as I slowly drag my feet to the door.

As soon as I open the door, I hear, "Noooo- don't!" before all the flashes take over my vision, and I am standing there completely shell shocked. Only to have Lucas and Winston run and jump in between me and the camera masses to push me inside, slamming the door behind us.

"Are you okay?"

"Ummmm, I am not really sure how to answer that. What the hell just happened? I was barely awake when I heard the knocking and thought maybe you left your key… Oh my gosh! Was that who I think those people are?" All he can do is nod yes to me as if he is trying to gauge my reaction, which turns into me completely flipping out. "What did I do? I am so sorry, Lucas, I am so so sorry. I ruined all this for you. I totally should have looked in the peep hole before opening the door. Oh my…"

"Breath, Emelia. Do not freak out. It will be okay, I promise. I need to call Kent right now. Stay right here." He takes charge as he gently pushes me onto the end of the bed to sit. He walks into the living room space, but I can hear his voice growing louder and angrier.

"I do not give a bloody hell about my image right now! Only about hers! Who the hell leaked this? Kent, this needs to be fixed right now! She was wrapped in a damn sheet when the cameras started flashing, and no, she is not fine. She is scared and worried to death about me of all people right now. I am jumping in the shower, and we will both be over there for the team meeting. Handle this!” Without even a look in my direction, he heads straight into the bathroom, and I hear the water turn on. Looking at the clock to see it is almost six-thirty, I realize a shower is not in my cards today, so I quickly dig a pair of jeans and my soft I love turtles Shelly Cove tee out of my suitcase to throw on. I throw my hair up in a pristine tight ponytail and wait for him to walk out. When he does, he stops for a split second like he wants to say something but doesn’t. Trying not to let him see me fall apart, I rush into the bathroom and slam the door and lock it.

“Emelia, let me in, we need to talk.”

I muster up, “busy,” and flip the faucet on so I can brush my teeth. While deciding that today is a good day for makeup to cover the bags under my eyes and help me put on my poker face for whatever is about to come. Once I feel like I have it together, I walk out only to run into a Lucas brick wall.

“Why the hell are you standing right at the doorway!?” I shout at him.

“Don’t you start. Emelia. Do not even. We will figure this out. I might not have handled the last twenty minutes right, but I am pissed. Not at you, but myself.”

“For what? You did not open that door, I did.”

“Because I should have put Rick up here to guard the door. I should not have taken Winston with me on the run, since everyone saw you with him yesterday. I should not have even…”

“Just say it. Just freaking say it, Lucas!” I yell as I punch him in the chest.

“I should not have brought you here. It was too soon. I should have waited until we were ready to be public with this. Because you will either be perceived as my latest one-night conquest, or we make everyone know the truth."

"Other than the world knowing about me, about us, and pissing off a few sponsors, what else are you not telling me that this is such an awful thing that happened? Don't get me wrong, the last thing I want is to be part of your tabloid stories or assholes thinking they can barge into my town and into my life, but what else is there?"

"I swear, Emelia, there is nothing else. I just wanted things to be different. I wanted you to meet my mum before the world did. I wanted my sisters and Dad to fall in love with you like I have. I wanted time for us to be us without the constant worry of cameras and reporters. I should have heeded Kent's warnings, but I hate being away from you, especially now that I will be crossing over both tours." Lucas places his palms on both sides of my face, pulling in for a kiss.

"I am not sure what the rest of the day will bring, but I promise you that leaving your side is not an option. At this point, if fans are pissed at me and sponsors are going bollocks, there is nothing left for me to do but to stand with you and be honest about us. You are not worth losing over any stupid plan they come up with to salvage this. Please tell me you understand, and you agree."
Not even able to look him in the eye, I say, "I will stand by you today, but do not ask me to stand by and watch you throw everything you have worked so hard away for me. That I will not do."

"Emelia…don't"

"No, Lucas, you don't. We will play this out until we can no longer. So let's get this over with," I say while grabbing his hand and leading him to the door. He soon pushes me up against the door frame, kissing me with the most vigor I have ever felt.

"With our foreheads touching, he whispers, "I will not lose you. This discussion is done."

Then he opens the door, pulling me out into the masses of cameras as we quickly walk down the hallway to the elevator avoiding the rapid-fire questions of who am I? Where did I come from? Playboy finally settling down? Until the elevator door finally closes, and we can breathe for a minute. With Lucas squeezing my hand, we exit the elevator on the ground floor, and luckily Rick and Kent are both there pushing the reporters out of the way, so we can make it to the black Cadillac untouched. Kent jumps in the back with us as Rick drives us over to the team area. We are all silent, and the tension is fierce.

<u>Lucas's POV</u>

We walk into the room hand in hand, with all eyes on us. Shockingly though, I see Shaun, one of the team owners, with a smile on his face as he gets up and walks over to shake my hand.

"About damn time, Stratton!" he cheers as he pats my back and then goes over to Emelia. "Welcome to the team, sweetheart. Anything you need, please reach out. Here is my card for safe keeping."

Emelia hugs him back and as she pulls away, she hesitantly speaks, "Thank you, Mr. Balfe. I really appreciate it."

"Please call me Shaun, and if my boy over here gets out of line, let me be the first one you call."
Smiling, she says, "Absolutely," as she gives off her nervous laugh.

"Can we please back up because I am lost after the bloody hell morning we have had."

Rob is the first one to speak, and I brace myself for his straight-shooting talk. "Well, son, we can tell you who leaked it in a moment, but first let's address the elephant in the room. You and her. I saw her in the garage yesterday and had my suspicions. After I had my wife gossiping with the women on the team, she declared what I thought was true. With that being said, we all could not be more than happy for you, but I am sure you will be hearing from Giacomo shortly about losing his best wingman," he states the last line with a laugh. "On a serious note, we have already reached out to CK, and as the photoshoots have happened with all the ladies, modeling is modeling, right?" I nod my head yes. "We have all agreed on your behalf that current shots are good to print and publish how and wherever they want. Especially since we are all under the assumption the two of you were already an item when those photo shoots happened over the last month." I know my head again in agreement. "You do have your Sport Illustrated interview this afternoon, so we need to decide if this is how you want to address the relationship. I can tell you they have already reached out, offering a nice price tag to get the exclusive on it. Money aside, this is also your personal life, so knowing all the details will somehow find a way to the world. I want you to make the decision about how it gets out there and setting the facts before all the rumors. We have all had to go through it at some point in our careers, luckily the hotter young guns that enter the circuit, the less they care about us old guys, so you have that to look forward to. So, thoughts?"

Looking at Emelia for some answer, she speaks up. "I am fine with whatever you decide and being able to control the narrative. I know nothing of how this half of people live and deal with society, so I trust in the decision you make."

"Easier said than done," I say to her while squeezing her hand in mine. "I say let us give the exclusive to SI. The interview comes at perfect time, and I trust and know the writer I am interviewing with to not debauch and twist anything."

"Good call, son," Shaun says. "He did state that he would push to have it printed this coming week in the bi-weekly print but will be online by tomorrow. Emelia, would you be able to stick around for the interview and possibly pose for some pictures if requested?"

"Um, if they need me to, but I will say I hope they don't." I can tell her whole body has tensed up, so I pull her up under my arm to hold her closer, rubbing her back.

"Our flight is together this evening, so she will be here, but let's try to avoid it if possible. Now can someone please tell me who leaked it, and the bigger question and as much as I appreciate it, why are my team owners handling my publicist duties instead of you?" We all turn to look at Kent, who has been eerily quiet since we walked into the room.

"Fine, it was me. I leaked it and led them to you, I…" I am across the room with my clenched fist slamming into his jaw before he can finish. "You mother- son of a bitch." As I go in for the second one, Lo and Pep are pulling me back. Rubbing his jaw, he looks square at me. "I was trying to make a point, but it clearly backfired."

"Oh, piss off! You fucking bugger. I could care less of your reasoning. I have trusted you with my brand, my life for the last twelve bloody years, and you have the audacity to try and make a point *with her*. Through all our discussions, not once have I turned down a gig you set up or endorsement deal. Is it because I told you that if there is an endorsement deal that does not accept me being in a relationship for I wanted no part of it?"

Kent looks at me with despair written all over his face. "I am sorry, man. I should have not played that card, and I do deeply regret it."

"I will have to deal with you later, but you better clean this mess up and get rid of all the reporters for the rest of the day. I must get on the track." Taking Emelia's hand, we walk out and down the steps to the garage area, where she sees Rick walking Winston around. Before she takes off to him, I pull her in, kissing the top of her forehead.

"There are not enough apologies for this shitshow of a morning, but I love you so damn much."

"I know you do." Though she doesn't say those three words back to me, I see it in her eyes. Because I have learned

those amber eyes show all her emotions regardless of her
intent to conceal them.

Chapter 24: Running Short on Lemons

If I thought this morning felt like an out of body experience, this afternoon contends to be even weirder. Kent managed to swipe the McClaren team area of all reporters along with throwing countless apologies at me. I feel like I have whiplash. Him hoping to use me to be put back in Lucas's good graces is very far-fetched for the moment. I still feel completely humiliated from being photographed in nothing but a sheet this morning and being used as a prop.

Even though Shaun has reassured me all the pictures have been bought and handled, there is still an uneasiness I have about one floating around somewhere. I guess time will only tell. I even sent Marcy a text letting her know what is going on and not to trust anyone we do not know coming into town. She said she would get with her boyfriend, Cliff, over at the precinct, to put plans in place at the main roads leading into town. Stating there is not much excitement for them these days, so they will be all over it in a heartbeat. At least I can be rest assured my little town will be safe, and the fact that if any unknown does make it in, they will be chased out. Now I am standing off to the side, watching the SI interview go down. They are doing it in the garage area to get some action and team shots, along with Lucas with his racecar. So far I have been left out of the interview, but I know it is coming. They even snuck some shots of Lucas and I earlier, while he had his racing suit hanging down around his waist, tied, with a tight white tee on with me in his arms looking up at him in the hot mess I showed up in earlier this morning. I'll admit it was a cute shot, but was not expected. Then right before the interview started, I caught the photographer taking pictures of Winston and me sitting down on the ground, trying to stay cool and out of the sun.

Lucas answers the questions like a pro. Several I catch are the typical repeat interview questions I have already heard or read about in articles, like favorite track, how did it feel to win such and such race, plans for the season, and how is the car handling? But I do hear some interesting new ones. Like:

Interviewer: Just want to know what was going through your mind when Mario did that slide job in turn four and you had to go low and slam on your brakes to avoid his car?

Lucas: All I am going to say is, we are teammates, but also competitors, and at the end of the day, I am not a fan of his. But I am sure he would say the same about me.

Interviewer: What are three songs or artists that you've been listening to lately?

Lucas: I would currently say Ryan Bingham who is an artist that was recently introduced to my playlist. Don't laugh, but Harry Styles is on my most listened to, and Five Finger Death Punch to get me amped up before hitting the track.

Interviewer: Aren't you proud? The interview is almost over, and I haven't asked you how important it is for you to win in the GT World Challenge here in America.

Lucas: (laughing) It is appreciated. Everyone around me knows I put more pressure on myself than anyone else could.

Interviewer: No one has ever seen you with an animal up until recently. Dogs or cats?

Lucas: I see where you are going with this… I am going with dogs. My sisters had cats growing up, but I absolutely prefer the companionship of a dog, especially a particular chocolate lab I know.

Interviewer: I am looking at this handsome lab off to my left being accompanied by a gorgeous lady. Would you be so kind in introducing them to the listeners and readers?

Lucas: Course. This here is my girlfriend, Emelia, and her dog, Winston. Though most think we met just over a month ago, we actually met a year ago in my hometown at a local pub.

Interviewer: Interesting. Did you keep in touch all this time?

Lucas: Actually no. I chatted with her for a bit, but then had to leave in a rush. Unfortunately, I never got her number and never thought I would see her again to be honest.

Interviewer: So, what you are saying is, fate has stepped in not only once, but twice now. Someone must really want the two of you together.

Lucas: I would agree, but she is way more than I could have ever dreamt of.

Interviewer: Now that the two of you are public to your world of fans, what are the plans during the season? Especially now that you are driving for both the American and European challenges.

Lucas: I foresee a great deal of travel in both of our futures. Emelia has her own career and life built, so trying to be respectful of her time. We will see where this season takes us and make plans for the future as we see fit.

Interviewer: This is for Emelia if you don't mind? Lucas turns to look at me, I nod, giving the okay.

Lucas: Sure, ask away.

Interviewer: Emelia, what do you think about this race world your boyfriend is part of?

Me: This realm is still so new to me, but it's intriguing. By nature, I am a slow paced person, but have such respect for him and any other person that can drive these cars to max speed while racing others on a track like this one trying to accomplish the same goal. It leaves me bewildered when watching Lucas and the drivers out on the track.

Interviewer: For all the disappointed women out there, how did you become "the one" to settle Lucas Statton down?

Me: That is the very question that I ask myself daily. I honestly do not have an answer for you.

Lucas: May I?

Interviewer: Of course.

Lucas: I knew she was the one when she did not squirt lemon juice in my eye after I destroyed her kitchen. *Everyone chuckles, and I am in shock he refers to that night.* No, but in all seriousness, she is the one because of who she is. Not only stunningly beautiful, but everything about her has me in awe and turns me on. She is easy to talk to and really listens. She has a sense of humor like no other. Beyond Jeopardy smart, but never makes anyone feel less of themselves. I easily annoy her, which is a huge highlight of my day because I also make her laugh, and bloke, she has the best laugh. Though she acts like she doesn't need me most of the time, I really know she actually does not because of how independent she is… I have completely embarrassed her, haven't I? *He asks while looking at me almost in tears and bright red.* I could go on about all the lush things about her, but I would also prefer to be the only one that can truly know and love her.

Interviewer: Well on that note, we can end the interview. I really appreciate you taking the time to chat, Lucas, and you too, Emelia. I know our readers and listeners have been waiting for this interview for a hot bit. Oh and here is a quaint gift basket for you both.

Me: Oh, thank you so much. I was running short on lemons. *Looking down at this lemon themed basket of soaps, an apron, a lemon cookbook, and actual lemons next to a bottle of lemon Moscato- what the actual hell!*

Lucas: My pleasure. It is always great to do interviews with you, man.

Finally, the recorder turns off, and I can breathe. After a few more photos are taken with Lucas and his car and team, SI leaves.

"You did great, darling," Lucas says, pulling me into a tight hug.

"Thank you, not too bad yourself, Mister Cool. Honest question though, can we go home now?"

"Home. I like the sound of that. And yes, my love, we can. Let me check in with the bosses and call Rick to pick us up." Giving me a kiss on the temple, he heads to the office above the garage.

Lucas's POV

We are finally home after one of the most stressful weekends of my life. Of course, sitting behind the year I almost lost the championship by one race where Alessondro spun me out, causing my car to slam into the barrier after sliding across the sand at over 130mph. I walked away unscathed, but the car was towed to the garage and had to watch the rest of the race from my motorcoach. The loss of points in that race hurt quite a bit, especially when the bad luck kept coming and could not even push into the top five for the next three races. So yes, I compare those weekends of my life as they could have been the most altering of situations.

Emelia was an ace dealing with all that shit today. The thought of losing her had me praying to all the Gods, even Eros, to provide some backup in keeping her with me. Now here we are laying in her bed, with her fast asleep on my chest, in my arms. Laying here preparing myself to conquer another day, another week, month, and my hopes for a lifetime with her. For me, this with her is home, and I have never envisioned myself homesick, until the thought of being away from her embodies my mind as I let exhaustion take over and fall to sleep.

"How frightening, that one person could mean so much, so many things."— Colleen McCullough, The Thorn Birds

Chapter 25: Wingman

It is Tuesday morning following the whirlwind of the weekend in Virginia. Sipping on my English tea with honey, I sit on the window seat, looking out to the clear blue sky with calm waves rolling in. Elated to be back home and back in the normalcy of my little town.

Marcy's boyfriend and deputies' office has done a great job on keeping outsiders like reporters out. Kent has managed to get back in and finagled a meeting with Lucas later this evening. Always trying to see the good in others, I am having a hard time myself staying angry with Kent as I do not honestly believe he was trying to be malicious and hurt Lucas or me. Though the fact is he did, and Lucas has trusted him for years, so I will be curious to know what the outcome will be. Lucas has not personally discussed it with me, since he has been making sure I am tended to since we arrived home. He seems to think I might shut-down due to all this nonsense and push him away. I won't lie either, as it has crossed my mind several times since Sunday. Bec has me talked out of it for now, so I let it lie in the back of my mind, ready to implement if and when the time comes.
I only have Lucas home this week before he leaves on Sunday night for race week. First race coming back from his hiatus and the season starting back up. He is under so much pressure, so I am trying to let him be and do as he wishes when it comes to helping me, extra cuddles, and being a sounding board. Even leaving him and Winston in bed to sleep for an extra hour or so because I feel him tossing and turning all night due to being so restless.

The sound of the doorbell pulls me out of my thoughts. *Who on earth could that be at nine in the morning?* Walking to the door, then looking through the peep hole, *because now I have learned my lesson,* a tall, sexy, jet blacked hair man is gracing my front porch. Slowly opening the door up because my curiosity has now gotten the best of me, I am greeted with the man pushing the door open with his strong arm and waltzing into my house like he owns it.

"Good morning, Bella, where can I find my dear friend Lucas?"

"Excuse me?" I blink as I am taken off guard. "Who are you? And you know there are laws that keep you from entering my home uninvited!"

Turning back to me like he could eat me alive, he smiles widely. "Bella, am I really not invited? I am your lover's best friend, his wingman."

"I honestly don't give a damn who you are?" At this time, Winston is barking to escape my bedroom since he heard the doorbell and now voices.

"Calm down, boy. Let's go. Darling, what are we doing for breakfast?" Lucas asks as he walks out of my bedroom, pulling a shirt over his head and making my inner workings throb for him. *You would think my ovaries would have enough by now.* I stay quiet, as he finally takes a look at me, as I move my eyes next to me, and he follows.

"Holy shit! G? What the bloody hell are you doing here, mate?"

"Me in the flesh. I had to come check on my boy and see what trouble he has been getting into since you have refused my calls several texts, and then I hear about your SI article from an interview I had yesterday morning. *Giacomo, how does it feel that your best wingman has fallen in love? Are you going to be the best man at the wedding?"* he asks himself in a very American voice, pretending to be the interviewer. Then reverting to his own self. "I do not know, Bob. If he is happy, I am happy for him. And of course, wherever he needs me to stand. I will always stand by Lucas." His face grows more serious, looking at me then back to Lucas. "What in the literal fuck is happening here? Are you playing house with her? She is beautiful, but again, what in the *fuck,* Lucas."

As much as I want to punch him for his language, he makes it sound so suave coming from his Italian mouth.

Though looking at Lucas, his jaw is ticking and body tense as if he is holding himself back from throwing a punch to Giacomo's pretty face.

"Back the hell off, G. Do not come into this house spouting off your bullshit like a twat. Sorry for not reaching out, but I have been laying low, and nobody is supposed to know where I have been. The bigger question is, how did you track me down?"

"Good Ol' Kent let me know because I would not stop bothering him. He is a such a sucker for a sob story on me missing my best guy and wanting to congratulate him."

"That idiot," Lucas mutters to himself. "G, I love you man, but walking in here like a damn tosser, makes me want to beat your arse."

"My apologies, amici. Let's start over please. Now will you please introduce me to this lovely woman in your life?"

Sighing, he looks back at me. "Emelia, please meet Giacomo. He drives for Ferrari and has been my wingman for a long time. G, meet Emelia, my girlfriend."

"You saying it puts me in a twilight zone…. But really, friend, I am pleased for you. For both of you. Just wish I was given a heads up before an interview."

"No, mate, I get it. I am sorry," Lucas says to his friend, punching him in the shoulder. Then they pull each other into a tight hug.

I literally think I just witnessed a bromance moment inside my house as if I was not even there. Clearing my throat after what seemed like several minutes of this man hugging, they turn to me with the realization they are no longer alone. Lucas, taking in my look of astonishment, comes over, putting his arm around me, then kissing me on top of the head.

"G, how long are you in town for?"

"Only till tomorrow night."

"Okay, let me take you over to the Airbnb where Kent is staying, and you can shack up there. We will be back, darling."

"Okay. How about after you guys get settled over there, you come for dinner, Giacomo. Right now, I need to get ready for work."

"That is kind of you, Bella, Thank you."

"You are welcome. And I will see you later." Leaning up to kiss Lucas on the lips, I whisper, "I'll go ahead and take Winston with me also."

"Okay, my love. I will check in later."
With that, I head to the bedroom to get dressed for the day, grab Winston, and we head out, all in a matter of twenty minutes. Before leaving, I caught a glimpse of the guys on the back deck talking and laughing over coffee. For me, this is going to be about trust and not letting all the articles I have read about the wingmen and their ladies cloud my judgment right now.

<u>Lucas's POV</u>

G and I get to the Airbnb to be met with a sorrowful Kent. He knows I am not happy he released my location to anyone, even if it is one of my closest mates. My own parents do not even know my exact location because I did not want them to feel pressured by possessing that knowledge when people ask. Then after meeting Emelia, it was even more prevalent to protect her and this town from all the outside drama. All I can do is shake my head in disbelief because this man in front of me keeps screwing up lately.

"G is staying with you through tomorrow."

"Sure, man. Whatever you need…… hey, are we going to discuss this weekend?"

I head to the fridge to grab a few beers and pass them out.

"Let's talk, and G can help me decide how to handle this. Because I am still bloody pissed at you."
Several hours of discussion, we finally came to terms. Kent understands he is on a tightrope with me but is staying on as my PR manager. I call Emelia to ask if it is okay if Kent comes to dinner also, and of course she is fine with it. The three of us head over, after G and Kent stop to grab some flowers for my girl and wine.

Dinner was splendid, of course, and after Emelia decided to head to bed, Kent also felt it was his time to head out before he became knowledgeable of our escapades. Kent prefers the denial method when it comes to handling any gossip or news. To him, unless he was there, heard about it, or there are pictures, *it never happened.*

After lots of laughs of some good times and future plots when back in Europe, G turns serious on me.

"Mate, tell me the truth. Did we just relive our glory days together because now you are a taken man?

"I believe so, G. Other than racing, I have never lived for anything or anyone else. But that woman in there makes me look at things differently. Almost as before I was looking through a telescope completely zoomed in on one planet, but she zoomed it out for me and showed me all that I had been missing."

G nods his head in acknowledgement.

"I know it sounds as if I am arse whipped, but one day you find the one that tilts your axis, and it will be all over for you. I promise… besides, we still have many glory days ahead of us, they just will not be including women for mc."

Both of us laugh. "Sounds good, Stratton. I hope you are right, and I am holding you to that. You are still my best wingman after all."

"Always, mate. Come on, it has been a long time since we binged movies together."

"Usual line up – remember? *Rush, LeMans, Ford vs Ferrari, The Italian Job, Talladega Nights to end it with Days of Thunder.*

"I'm droppin' the hammer!" we both shout in unison. I will apologize to Emelia in the morning for all the shouts, laughs, and quoting that will transpire throughout the night into the early morning.

After an entertaining dinner with the guys, it became the mission of Lucas and his *mate,* to educate me on racing and cars. I was awakened at five this morning to be dragged out of my warm cozy bed to begin watching old racing videos of theirs from tracks around the world. Barely able to keep my eyes open, I try hard to absorb some of what they are throwing at me.

Lucas: "See here, that is what you call the banking. It is when the angle at which a track inclines toward the outside of a corner or from the lower to the higher side of a straight away.

Giacomo: "Okay, you see him coming in for a pit stop on pit lane. Meaning having the pit crew put on tires or corrections to the car in a matter of seconds. Here, look. That is an air jack, this guy has an air impact wrench to quickly get the tires on and off. Here. Watch how fast these guys complete a pit stop with tires and gas."

Lucas: "Oh, check out this hairpin on this track. It is a tight 180-degree corner that twists back on itself. Here it flows right back into the racing line, which is the fastest circuit of the track… This is a great shot of the inside of the car. See all these bars inside my car? This is called a roll cage. It is exactly what it stands for and gives great protection. Also, my seat is tightly fitted to my body as well as my harness is specially made for me to keep my neck and head in one place instead of bouncing everywhere when in wrecks.

Giacomo: "Oh shit, is this the race where you bumped the pace car? HA, it is. See, Bella, the pace car comes out to slow everyone one down and causes the cars to tighten back up and realign. Pace car comes out at the start of a race, and then when we have yellow and red cautions. Your lover over here likes to give the pace car a hard time." They both have been talking nonstop for hours along with laughing and reminiscing.

Around eight AM , I beg them to stop as my head is spinning with terms from camber, wrench, shocks, horsepower, McLaren to Ferrari features, followed by world renowned tracks. I promise each of them I will pull some books while at the library today to read up on. Also reminding Lucas, we have Blues on the Beach again, so I will see him later. Getting up to get dressed in my bedroom, my phone rings in my hand.

"Morning, Bec."

"Morning, my peach. How is it going?"

"I feel like I have been babysitting two grown men for the last twenty-four hours, who are excited to teach me about race cars with as much enthusiasm as a five-year-old on Christmas morning. Send help. Please."

Laughing at my predicament, she says, "Oh my gosh, can I send the hubs your way to babysit also? He would love that."

"No, Bec. Did you not hear me? Send Help!"

"You know you love it. Him bringing you into his world."

"I do, but it is a lot. And then there are two of them as they veer off on sidebar conversations, leaving me more lost than I was before. It is interesting and cool as shit. Ugh, I am just angry and horny and need to be done complaining."

"Problems with lover boy?"

"I don't know. We haven't made love since Saturday night in Virginia because he has just been treating me like I might break or run screaming for the mountains. Then mister bestie showed up yesterday, and though he was to sleep at the other house with Kent, he ended up crashing here because they stayed up till four in the morning and proceeded to pull me out of bed at five to start my crash course. Now it is Wednesday, I am off to work with a long day and a concert that I have to be at tonight, followed by just complete exhaustion."

"Hang in there, girl. Make the best of it today and then jump him like a rodeo bull tomorrow night once the bestie travels back overseas and you have time to rest. But you also need to talk to Lucas. He needs to not treat you like fragile glass because you are far from it.”

“I know, but he is already so stressed about next week and trying not to add to his stress.”

“Did you stop to think you might be helping with his stress, if he knows he does not need to worry about you so much.”

“Oh, good point. Damn. I know I keep you around for a reason.”

“Of course, and besides, no one loves you more than me.”

“You are the best! And only one and half more weeks until you are here with me”

“Counting down, and you know my mom already has a schedule and meals planned.”

“I expect nothing less. Alright well gotta run, or I will be late opening today. Love you, Bec.”

“Love you, talk to you later.”

Bec is right, I need to talk to him, so I am one less thing he needs to be thinking about next week at the track. He has bigger fish to fry than worry about little ol’ me.

Lucas’s POV

It is about seven in the evening, and I am heading over to the beach to watch the concert with Emelia. I sent G off with a promise to be better about letting him know the *scoop* before anyone else does. I have missed him, and I can tell the fans are loving the selfie we posted on his Instagram of us together. Wondering what mischief we could have possibly been getting into, along with everyone wondering where we are.

Walking up to our original spot up on the dunes, I spot Emelia and Winston playing frisbee with Oliver and a few of his friends, as they wait for the concert to start.

Sneaking up behind her, I grab her by her waist twirling her around, causing her to scream in panic then into a full-on giggle when she realizes it's me.

Bending down, I lock my lips on her sweet ones, then pull back. "I have missed you, darling."

"I have missed you too," she mumurs as she brings her arms up around my neck, pulling me closer to her for a longer sensual kiss.

"Ewwww, really, Mister Lucas?"

"Sorry not sorry, Oliver. I love her too much to keep my hands and lips off of her."

"Gross…. I think I hear my mom calling. See you tomorrow, Miss Emelia."

"Good night, Oliver. Now, where were we?" She pulls me back down for another kiss.
"I think I need to take you directly home and have my way with you."

Giving me a wink, she says, "I like that idea, but we can't leave just yet. Come, let's sit and enjoy. At least until Marcy gets here since she is taking over the cleanup tonight." I quickly pick her and carry her over to our spot, with Winston tight on my heels and barking at us.

"Looks like I am not the only one missing your undivided attention the last couple of days," she states, laughing. As soon as I sit down in my chair, Winston is up in my lap, thinking he is the size of a chihuahua but far from it. Keeping Emelia's hand in my right, I hold and scratch Winston with my other hand.

"Hey can we talk?" I hear her ask. My mind begins to go in a million directions and scenarios because when has it ever been a good outcome when a woman says those words.

"Floor is yours."

"I am just going to come out and say it, so please do not get mad or jump to interrupt me. I just need you to hear." Emelia looks at me intently, before taking a deep breath. "I know you love me, but part of you loving me I think is how strong and independent you think I am. But since this past weekend, you have been walking on eggshells around me and treating me like fragile glass. I want to tell you I am not fragile. I know I have a history, and I do not like being pushed into anything and the thought of being thrusted into the spotlight next to you makes me want to vomit. Like seriously vomit. But Lucas, I am okay right now. I am taking these changes in stride. My trust is in you to protect me, yet you cannot hover over me like you have been. Stressing over me is worthless because, by now, you should know I will come out on the other end just fine. So, stress about your car, the upcoming race or races. Stress about what you are eating for breakfast in the morning and all the travel you will be doing. Stress about everything except me. I love you, but I will not be handled as if I will break."

I quickly take her face in my palms and kiss her, then pushing my forehead against hers.

"Come home with me after next week's race. After V.I.R, I must head out to Belgium for the Spa-Francor champs for a mid-week race. We can leave right after for me to take you home to meet my mum and family. I know it was not planned for you to come to that race, yet it could not be better timing, and I know she is dying to meet you."

"Let me think on it. As it is short notice, and I have Bec and her family coming up the last week in June."

"Please say yes. I will have you back in time for them, and I will be heading back on the third right after my race is over in Italy. Then I'm home until Watkins Glen followed by another Belgium race."

"Sure, why not. Let me clear this with Marcy and Mrs. Baxter first."

I quickly stand up, placing Winston on the ground, then pull her up in my arms to hug her tightly. Getting her in my hometown for my mum to see how wonderful she is and my sisters to make her feel like family is everything to me right now. For me, it is the next step in our relationship and giving her a family of people that will love her as their own, which I know deep down she longs for. Holding her tighter to me, I whisper, "I am keeping my promise to make sure those sad eyes keep shining and you feel and know your place in this life, my darling." Kissing the top of her head, never wanting to let go of her, a coldness wash over me when she steps out of my embrace.

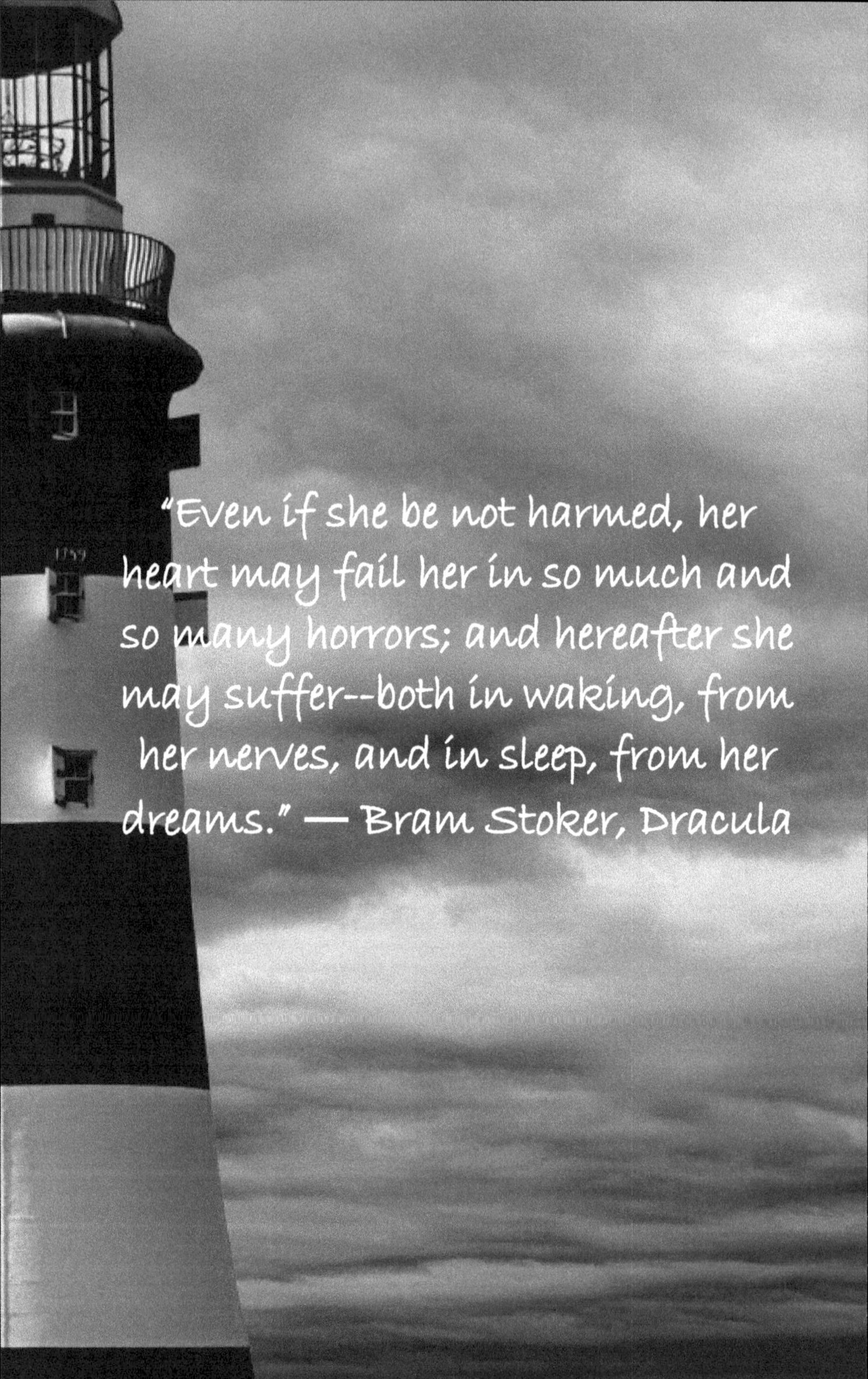

"Even if she be not harmed, her heart may fail her in so much and so many horrors; and hereafter she may suffer--both in waking, from her nerves, and in sleep, from her dreams." ― Bram Stoker, Dracula

Chapter 27: To Dream a Dream

My nightmares have been heavy over this last week. So much so, Lucas tries to sing me to sleep, sex me to death to over exhaust me to even fighting his own exhaustion, thinking that if I talk through them with him, I will overcome them. My constant struggle is how do you overcome a *thing* that happened in reality. Most nights I am shaken awake by Lucas because I am crying and screaming in my sleep. As if my subconscious is trying to release the emotions, I should have had through all of it, instead of suppressing them. It would be one thing if my nightmares consisted of Freddy Kreuger coming up through my sheets and pulling me into his world, or being caught in an actual tornado, to maybe even the horror of a car accident. Yet, they are not. I fall asleep to be brought back to the last few days before my mama passed. To our last actual dinner and conversation together. Discussing the future as if she was going to be around to bare witness to all of it. Like wedding plans for example. I hate the fact that she died with the notion Connor and I were getting married and starting a family. Or even the notion that I was okay with this damn decision she had made.

It starts with the Saturday I go and pick her up from her house. My dad was out of town working, and as if she planned it while he was gone, it was her que to leave. Not wanting to put the burden on him, and after about a week of no dialysis, she was to the point of worsening where hospice could step in. Mama refused to have hospice at the house, so we opted for inpatient hospice at the hospital, which we had to wait until a certain point with her health.

You know the feeling of taking your beloved dog or favorite pet to the vet to put down because they are ill or old age. That feeling of guilt, remorse, and heartbreak, knowing that pet is not coming back home with you alive. That recognition of your home will be forever altered, and you are losing a loved one? That is what I felt, picking her up, taking her to the hospital to get checked in. As she sat there and went over her to-do list and things, I needed to remember on the ride over. Once to the hospital, trying to get checked in was a nightmare. The providers kept pulling my sister and I aside about us agreeing to our mama's wishes, how she was so young to be going through this. Is she of sound mind? I think at one point the staff was wondering if any of us were of sound mind, but with a quick rundown of all her medical problems and conclusion of no transplant, they relented and finally admitted her under Hospice care. Then it became a waiting game. We had a few days of laughs, conversations, and good meals.

I remember coming in on a Wednesday while she was asleep, and I could hear the crackle sound her lungs were making as she breathed. They were filling with fluid, and Hospice let me know she was getting closer to the end as her body was fulfilling its duty to naturally shutdown. Even assured me she was in no pain, even though it sounded like she might be. Known as the death rattle, it still haunts my ears as I listened to it for two days on and off. My sister and I took turns with her, making sure she was never alone. Knowing our time was becoming more limited.

It was Friday afternoon when I stopped by, holding her hand for a bit. Mama was pretty out of it, so I thought it was the perfect time to have a mini breakdown. Crying, letting her know how much I loved her, and I was not ready for her to be gone. Not ready for her to miss out on so many more life's milestones and to face this world without her guidance. That I was questioning myself in supporting her life altering decision in its final hours. With a squeeze of my hand, she softly spoke in a gurgling whisper, "I am sorry." Which only made me feel guilty and had me apologizing for the next thirty minutes and convincing both of us I was not angry with her. That I still understood the bigger picture. All I got was another gentle squeeze.

My sister came up in the evening, and we sat around her bed reminiscing some childhood stories and the last few weeks with Mama. Joking how awkward Thanksgiving was, like it was the *final supper.* We talked about upcoming trips and plans for Christmas and the New Year. The promises Mama made us make, like living our lives as if she was still here with us. To be the daughters she raised and not let this knock us down. The promise I had to make to keep tabs on my dad. Check-in with him and make sure he was fine when she passed. The promises my sister had to make with her, which I am sure had to do with me and being happy and content with her life moving forward.

When we left that night, hospice had us hoping we had until Sunday, so the plan was to meet back up there in the morning, because the last thing we wanted was her to be alone when she passed. The next morning, she was gone.

Chapter 28: Another Storm

Another storm rolled in last night causing a sleepless night and uneasiness settling in the pit of my stomach. Lucas leaves this afternoon to head out to Virginia for the week. This only makes me more antsy with my emotions. Something is brewing, not only in the sea, but in this reality surrounding me. I feel it in my heart, my leg, my whole body to be exact. Checking out the weather, it looks like it will be a week of storms, with an impending hurricane swirling around out in the Atlantic. Luckily for Lucas, Virginia should have clear skies all week.

I have had to constantly reassure Lucas that I will be fine. Reminding him that I lived in sea town all my life, and that I will be with him come Friday to watch him race. That all his focus is to be on racing and getting rest where he can because he has a race next mid-week across the pond. Lucas makes me giggle every time I say pond in this reference because he shouts "massive ocean" back to me. Regardless of if I think he hears me or not. One of our many new jokes we have established over the last month. These next two weeks are going to be harsh. The weekend schedule will be me seeing him post race and early mornings. Sunday after the race, I will fly back home as he heads out to Belgium. Then I will fly into London to meet him for the weekend to meet his family before he jets off to Italy for the Misano race, and again, I head back home a lonely girl.

Winston already has a sense of something amidst as well. Lucas is all packed and about to head out the door, as my suitcase still lies on the floor half-packed. He is a quick study when he does not see his travel bag out to be packed.

"Darling, I am off. Kent is here," Lucas shouts from the front door. "Are you coming to see me off?'

I have been scrubbing the grout in the kitchen tile for the last hour because of my nerves, and I am sure I smell like bleach. Washing my hands and rushing to meet him at the door, he meets me in the hallway, snatching me up in his arms and pressing our bodies into each other.

"You, my darling, I am going to miss very very much," he states as he kisses my entire face and neck, making my laugh.

"Not as much as I will miss you, Mister Cool." Giving him a sensual kiss on his lips to hold on to until Friday. "Be careful and let me know when you land."

"I will." After he bends down to rub Winston's ears, telling him to be a good boy, then stealing one last kiss from me, he walks out the door.

Back to scrubbing the grout it is.

Lucas's POV

Finally, it is Thursday, and it already has been an exhausting week. Not just because Emelia is not by my side, but between team meetings, driver meetings, and threatening the crew not to alter anything on my car because other than tires, I left it perfect when I exited the car a week ago. Tomorrow is official practice, then qualifying on Saturday with Sunday being the actual race. It is my job to not botch the car between now and then. Steady fast lines, not to quick at the turns, staying in front of the grouped drivers, and watching the road ahead of me.

Practice day is here. My American teammate Braun and I go out in the next slot so we are geared up and ready to jump in, but not until we hear Beretta's time in the Lamborghini Huracan. *Bolloks!* Best lap of the day so far and pole position if he does it again tomorrow with a time of 1:45:750 with Ferrari not far behind at 1:46:232. Time to show what this McLaren team can really do, and what I can do with this beautiful badarse of a race car. Lo talks to me through my headset.

"Lap one: Warm up: Go easy on her now. Clocked-1:47:032. Just warming up those tires."

"Lap two: Steady around turn 4, make it up in the straightaway. Clocked- 1:46:456. Getting closer."

"Last three: All you Stratton. Clocked-1:46:012. Not too shabby, give that big girl some love for me."

"10-4, Lo. She is handling like a dream," I say back. Pulling into the pits knowing my time out there, knowing I had more to give, my gut told me to hold back a bit, so I did. The team and I feel ecstatic about the times, and Braun's fastest lap was at 1:45:767. I know he has room to push harder, but today is just practice. Tomorrow we push our limits for the heater lap and see where that places us in the lineup. Now that practice is over, time to shower and clean up for the team dinner tonight. Checking my phone, I see I have a missed text from Emelia.

Emelia - **Hey, Mister Cool. Flights are delayed due to the storm worsening, but no need to worry. Winston and I are snuggled in at the house with Marcy and her boyfriend. Town still has power, for now. Hate I could not make it out today, but as of right now, I have a flight booked for Sunday morning to make it to the race at least. I know you are busy, so just text or call when you can. Missing you. -XO   E**

Me: **Just got off the track and saw your message. It saddens me that you are not here in my arms, but please remain safe and sound where you are. We will play Sunday by ear. I will not risk your safety to be here. Have to get ready for the team dinner. Will call you later tonight. Miss you most, my darling. – LS**

Even with Emelia not by my side at dinner, she was still the topic of conversation. The owners' wives wanted to know more about her, the team and crew swooned over her. I honestly cannot wait to let her know how much she was missed tonight, as I know she has won over so many with her personality and beauty already, but will soon win all hearts over. Once in my room for the night, I make a call to her. She enlightens me to the fact that all power is out currently on her end of the town and cell signals are not the best. Making our conversation hit or miss. I am able to tell her I love her, with her common response of stay safe and miss you, before she quickly hangs up before I can say another word. I let it be. She will tell me she loves me in her own time. I just wish I could at least glance in her eyes to know the feelings are there.

Chapter 29: Breaking

After waking up late to catch my flight, weaving through fallen trees and debris, I made it to my gate at the airport with ten minutes to spare. His race is at two o'clock, and I finally land at eleven this morning, post another delay on landing here in North Carolina due to the east coast storms battering up the coastlines and pushing inward.

Once on the ground, I turn my phone on to text Lucas, I made it. Knowing at this point he is probably jamming out to his old school iPod, getting pumped for the race. Leaving no expectation that I should hear back from him, so I am excited to surprise him post race. Following my sent text to Lucas, my phone starts pinging off the rails with texts and missed calls. Not recognizing the number and for some reason my voicemail did not want to load, I click the app to see several text messages from the same number. Odd.

Unknown number: **Emelia, please give me a call ASAP. It is about your dad.**

The uneasiness and dread I have been feeling all week rises to the back of my throat. On the flip side, I cannot believe this bitch had the nerve to contact me. Staring at my phone for several minutes while the plane pulls up to the gate, I decide to call back the number, all the while preparing myself for that woman's voice I cannot stand, and I need to keep composure since I am still on a plane. I brace myself for when the phone stops ringing, and there is an answer.

"Hello… Emelia?" A sweet voice comes over the phone.

"Hi, this is Emelia. Who is this?"

"This is Danielle, your dad's girlfriend." I am completely taken back from her words, thrown off by her voice, but realize she is crying.

"Oh, okay. You are definitely not who I was preparing myself to talk to… Sorry, what is going on with my dad?"

Full on sniffles and tears falling is all I hear on the other end.

"I do not know how else to tell you this, but he is gone. He passed away sometime last night, early this morning."

"Um…what? He is gone?" The blood leaves my face, and I begin shaking trying to understand the words she just told me.

"Yes. He was not feeling well all weekend, and I tried so hard to get him to go and get checked out, but he just refused to go to the hosptial." I release a chuckle from my throat. Getting my dad to the doctor is near impossible, let alone the hospital. "I just loved him so much, and I hate that I am talking to you for the first time like this. I am really so sorry."

"Yah, I am also sorry for your loss. Again sorry, I am really not sure what to say right now. He is the man that was never supposed to die, let alone, he disappeared on me over a year ago. And he obviously is not where or with who I thought he was. Where are you located?"

"We are living in Pensacola. We bought a house about two years ago. Honey, can I call you back? My son just got here, and we are waiting on the EMS and coroner to arrive.

"That is fine. I need to call my sister anyways. I will talk to you later."

My every being is trying to push down the tears that threaten to fall. My emotions are exploding as I dial my sister. She is in much shock as I am when I share the news, and even though they had more of a distant relationship then him and I did, at the end of the day, it is the realization that our father is gone. That in our mid-adult life, we are orphaned, parent-less. The anger of him dying peacefully in his sleep when our mama had to stretch it out over a week begins to fume. Not to mention all the pain and suffering Mama had prior. The realization that he had a girlfriend that was not Sheryl and a whole other life all the way down in Florida that we were not privy to is obscene. I leave her to wrap her mind around the news with the promise of calling her when I know more. My next call is Bec. She may be my only lifeline to process any of this and figure how to just get back home and deal.

"Hey, E, you headed to the track?"

"Bec… Bec, he is gone. My dad is dead." Just saying those words out loud makes me numb to even moving. Panic starts to set in as the plane is unloading, and I have no idea what I am supposed to do or where I am supposed to be.

"Oh, baby girl, no. Okay. Where are you right now?"

"Um, I am about to get off the plane. Bec, I need to get home."

"I got you. E, walk to the front of the plane and hand over your phone to the nicest flight attendant you see." I begin walking down the aisle, sweating, and analyzing the attendants and stop at the one right in front of the cockpit and just hand her my phone. She looks at me like I have lost my damn mind, which I do not blame her but motioning my phone to her again, she takes it and holds it up to her ear. I see her eyes looking me over, and a sense of pity graces her face. Once she hangs up and hands me the phone back, she takes my arm in hers, and we begin the descent through the walkway to the airport.

"Emelia, your friend is going to call you back in ten minutes. In that time, I am going to take you over to the service desk and get you on the first flight back this afternoon, okay?"

Nodding my head in acknowledgement, I feel like I am an autopilot. The service desk was nothing but kind and sufficient in booking me on a two o'clock flight back home, and Bec is on time with her callback.

"Hey, E. Tell me your flight number and time." I read it to her. "Okay, I am heading to the airport now and will meet you at your gate and will be taking you home. Stay on the phone with me, and I want you to go to the Sky Club to grab a drink and some food. And we are going to stay on the phone as long as we can, okay?"

"Okay. Going now." Once settled in at sky club with a Bulleit on the rocks. I sigh.

"Bec, what am I going to do? I am officially an orphan. O my god, he wanted to be buried in his family plot. I am not sending his body back. Will he care if I cremate him? Shit, Mama was supposed to be buried with him. I need to call Grandma; she needs to know."

"E… E… Emelia! I need you to breathe. There is nothing you need to do right now. We will figure all this out once I get you home."
Time passes as she keeps me on the phone with the latest Ella shenanigans and our upcoming trip in the fall.

"Wait, I need to call Lucas. No, I can't. He is getting ready to race. He does not need to hear about this until after his race."

"I got you. E. I have already sent him a text. All I said was that the flight was delayed and to call when the race was over."

"Okay, good. Thank you. What would I do without you, Becca? You are my family."

"Anytime, and you are doing great right now. You finished with your drink?"

"Yes."

"Okay, let's get you on that plane to head home."

Once on the plane, I decide to text Danielle.

Me: **Hi, Danielle, this is Emelia. Just wanted to let you know I am on a flight headed back home. I will reach out once home and settled to touch base on everything.**
Danielle: **No problem, honey. Safe travels home. They just came and picked up his body, and I went ahead and asked for an autopsy.**
Me: **Sounds good, and I am so sorry you are having to handle this and for your own loss.**

Bec is right where she says she would be when I disembark the plane. I collapse in her arms. Partly because I had five too many drinks on the plane, other part I feel like I am breaking into pieces all over again.

Lucas's Epilogue:

I managed a time of 1:45:016 on my heater lap yesterday in qualifying, putting me second to the pole leader at a lap time of 1:44:765. The Lamborghini is going to be in my front view until I find him in my rearview. I am pumped up now sitting in the car, focused on the goal at hand. Ready for the greenlight. No distractions, just me and my McLaren baby racing for the finish line. Green flag dropped - We are off.

"Keep it steady, man. You have ten second lead over third. Braun is pushing past fifth to catch up to you hopefully here soon. You are two seconds behind Beretta," Lo talks into the headset.

"Eight laps down, man. Thirty-six more to go."

"Is Emelia there?"

"Did you just ask that? Where is your focus, man? But no, I do not see her. Kent was on the phone with Rick earlier, so I am sure she is around somewhere."

"I know, Lo. I think she is the one thing that can penetrate this focused mind. She just came to my thoughts. Refocused in.

"Am I good to push this round? Where is the lap traffic?"

"Now or never, speed racer." Coming out of turn twelve, I lay the hammer down, topping off at 190 mph as we approach turn thirteen, and I slingshot in front of him. *Got him!*

"That's what I am talking about, speed racer. That's what I am damn talking about!"
I am keeping at least a second ahead of him, but I sense him closing in. With ten laps to go, it is going to be a close finish for sure.

"Okay, man, you got Braun on the other side of Beretta. Let's win big for the Privé."

With two laps to go, Beretta gets on the inside enough to push my car over and takes the lead. Finished results were

Beretta, myself, then Braun. Still an amazing win for the Privé McLaren team. Post podium pictures and sprayed champagne, I was nervous as I did not see Emelia anywhere. I wanted her to run up to the podium and hug me. I have missed her so much. Back in the garage, where things are a little less chaotic, I find Kent to ask him where Emelia was. He was very quick to say her flight was delayed again and did not make it. Not thinking too much about it with the storms the town has had lately, I head to my cubby for my phone to check in with her, wondering if she watched it on TV then and to read any texts she sent.

"Where in the bloody hell is it?" I mutter to myself after tearing apart my bag and area.

"Missing something, mate?" Pep asks as he walks on by.

"Yes, my bloody phone. It was right here with my iPod when I geared up."

"I don't know, mate. Hope you find it, or you are going to have one beautiful woman pissed at you." Smirking at each other, I acknowledge what he said is true. I go back to digging for my phone. I only have an hour before we head to the airport for Belgium.
With no luck in any of my bags or gear or garage area that I personally had every one turn upside down, I go to Kent.

"Kent, I need to borrow your phone please."

"Where is yours?"

"Are you a damn twat? Have you not been paying attention that it has been missing?" He only looks at me with a blank stare.

"No can-do buddy. Waiting on an important call for an interview time. Besides, we need to load up and head to the airport. Rick is waiting."

"Bloody….ugh! A phone does not have legs and just walks off!" I shout.

Now throwing whatever I can get my hands on, eyes go wide around me with nervousness and fear. Lo quickly rushes to my side and hands me his phone. I quickly call my voicemail to hear Bec's voice that I should call when I can, but flight was delayed, and Emelia was at home. I find it very peculiar that Bec is leaving me a voicemail and not Emelia herself. My "spidey-senses" as Emelia jokes are pinging everywhere. Something is bizarre, and I never thought to memorize her damn number because of stupid technology that is always linked to me. *Cloud.* I need access to my cloud. I take note that my crew is loading up for the airport, and I need to do the same. I am riding with Kent who is refusing to give his phone up, and Rick stating he needs his for navigation. I honestly have never felt so panicked and useless not having a phone in my hand to check on the one person I know needs me right now.

As if the world is completely against me, we barely make it to the flight on time. *Great!* Knowing there is nothing I can do, I sit back and plug up to watch a movie as we take off. Thirty minutes after take-off the flight attendants begin to make their rounds for refreshments. I go ahead and order two Jacks neat, knowing I am going to down them as soon as they are placed in front of me. When she comes back, she keeps staring at me, and as I give her a side eye and a look, she speaks up at a whisper.

"Hi. I don't want to cause a scene, but you are Lucas Stratton, right?"

"Last I checked." Not in the mood for games but in a cocky mood to say the least.

"Oh, well, my boyfriend is a race fanatic and follows you. Says he thinks you will be joining the F1 series by next season. Is there any way I can get you to autograph this napkin for him?"

"Tell your boyfriend thanks for the boost of confidence. And sure." I squiggle my name on the napkin and hand it back to her.

"Also, I hope your girlfriend is okay. My boyfriend told me it was on the news about her missing your first race."

"Thank you. She is fine, her flight was delayed." The attendant freezes in place and looks at me as if I am off my rocker. Her eyes narrow at me.

"Miss, if you have something to say, just say it."

"Um, well I was just going to say there is no point in lying, because those that listen to the GT podcasts and racing news already know."

"Know what exactly?" I grind out with my eyes narrowing back at her and feeling like my breath is starting to be slowly sucked out of my body.

"That she had a panic attack on the plane because she just received word her father had passed."

The air has been sucked out of me. I can no longer breathe in or out. I can no longer see straight. I feel as if I am having an out of body experience, and all is in slow motion around me.

"Sir… Sir… are you okay? Here breathe into this bag." I breathe out but cannot seem to catch my breath. "I am so sorry, Mister Stratton. I thought you knew. Um, here. Here is the quick snippet my boyfriend sent me earlier." She pushes play. I recognize the voice of Stan from the GT podcast instantly.

"It was a huge day for the Privé team, with Stratton and Braun claiming the second and third spots on the podium next to Baretta today. Even with this great accomplishment in the McLarens, all of it was overshadowed today by one big question. *Where was Lucas Stratton's girlfriend?* Did not take long for rumors to spread that our favorite playboy was up to his old habits again, or even as far as stating the girl was no true match for him and the racing world. O' wait we have a caller. – Hello Caller, can you offer some insight into where the girlfriend was today."

"Yes, I was on the flight with her to North Carolina. She looked to be having a nervous breakdown once we landed. I sat several rows back but tried to eaves drop as best as I could. Gosh, I know that sounds awful, don't hate me

people, I am only human. Once off the plane, I approached the lady that was sitting behind her, and she stated from what she could tell, Emelia just got word from some woman she did not know that her father had passed."

"Well then. Thank you, nosy Betty, for the information and sharing. If this is true, this means she was meant to be at the track today, but my deepest condolences go out to her and her family during this time. Now I am interested to know if Stratton will be taking time off or if we will be seeing him behind the wheel at Belgium this week."

Fuuuuuuck! I just keep repeating that word, until I have exhausted all my *fucks* for the hour. All I want to do right now is land this damn plane myself. Instead, I must sit here for the next ten hours in agony before we touch down. Kent will be lucky if I do not throw him out of this plane before we land, because my lack of a phone has him written all over it. Ten hours. A series of events can happen in ten hours. A series of emotions thinking I left her and what a bastard I am can happen in ten hours. Becoming a threat to herself if she is not handling this well can happen in ten hours. I lean my head back in the seat and close my eyes. Trying to not think of the if's right at this moment, but how her haunting amber eyes have shined since our time together.

Daddy. Who would have thought at this point in our lives you would be gone? Though you disappeared on me, you remained in the back of mind. Waiting for the phone call or visit where you apologize for leaving. Be a man who admitted that he was wrong for so many reasons, and you carried the guilt with you for all of it. Knowing I will never be over my mama's death, I am now faced with yours. So much left unsaid from the both of us, causes me angst. It made my heart soar when I heard you talked about me, about us to your girlfriend. That it seemed you even missed us. But soon, the anger and resentment filled my heart back up, due to you being too stubborn to pick up the phone. That you thought you could take off one day and disappear and not have to face the heartbreaking melody we all find ourselves with. Not going to lie, I am pretty damn pissed that you accomplished it too. I used to be daddy's little girl, and I wonder if you still thought of me that way. I inherited your dark features, your olive skin, love for history and books, the love for travel, along with the mouth of a sailor. You also gave me my trust issues and a reason to hate. I will always love you, but please give me time on my path to forgiveness. It is a long, rugged dark one.

Also, I would appreciate it if you told your red cardinal self to f-off. Over the stalking and random attacks. Thanks!

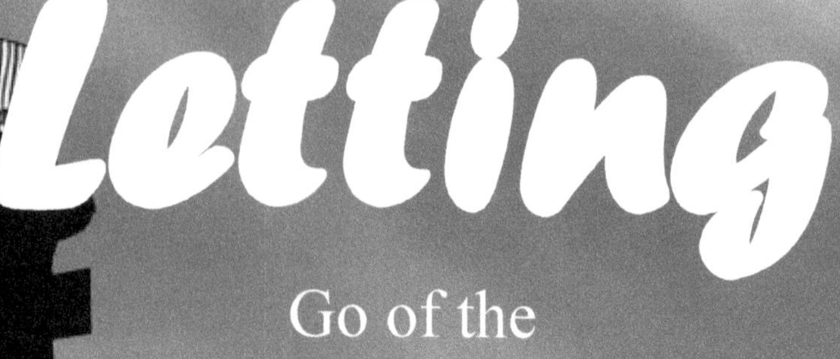

Letting
Go of the
Storm

By Ali Marie

Book 2 of 2- Storm Series

Bec's Perspective

It has been hours since I got her home, showered, dressed in pjs, and into bed. The only movement she makes is to dry heave into the trashcan I placed by her bedside. My person is unraveling at the seams, and I am not sure what to do to stop it. The shock over her father's death is consuming her. The duck not quaking about her lover boy not reaching out has still been heard loud and clear. I might even murder him myself if she does not.

I have been on the phone with this random Danielle lady off and on. She told me what happened, and her thoughts on the cause of death. She filled me in on who she was and their relationship, as well as cluing me in that she knew a lot more than I gave that man credit for when it came to sharing. Danielle said he was very open about the life he gave his family, the awful mistress, how sick his wife was, and all the guilt he carried with him. Memories of his daughters growing up, the life's they were leading, and how proud he was of them both. *That mother fuckerer of a man.*

I had to stand by and watch Emelia spiral after he vanished and having to deal with her prick of a fiancé. Connor was good for E in the beginning. I liked how he made her feel safe and wanted, but overtime I could see something shift. After her mama died, Connor's true colors were shown, and I knew he would never be enough for her. He could never provide my girl with the love and life she deserved.

For her father, I grew up watching E be daddy's little girl. She could get away with anything in his eyes, and he always made sure to give her whatever she asked for. Even in the hardest times, he made things happen for her. When she grew up and came to know the truth behind the longest affair in history, she somehow forgave him or just ignored it and went on being daddy's little girl. Then when her mom passed, she only found anger and resentment towards him. She would check on him as her mama had asked from time to time and be pleasant, but that was the extent of it. When he left, she was pissed he took away whatever shelter or support he gave her despite everything she hated about him and the situation. He took away the promise she had made to her mom. He took away the last of her physical connection when he took away the voicemail message. I did at least make her a quilt out of all her mom's clothes that she left her, that she is now tightly wrapped on in resting.

Seven in the morning, I roll over to see Lucas's name pop up on my phone. *Son of a bitch.* I roll out of bed and sneak out of Emelia's room, casting one last glance at her to make sure she is still asleep. I answer my phone.

"You sorry bastard. I should not have even answered the phone, but I need a viable reason to tell my girl where the hell you have been. And I really hope you have been in hell."

"Becca! For the love of all things holy, please let me talk. I deserve everything you want to throw at me. I will not argue that. Just first, let me know how she is doing?"
It takes everything for me not to cuss and scream at this man.

"How do you think she is doing?"

"I can imagine miserable, but that is why I am damn well asking, Bec."

"Nailed it! Anything else I can help you with?"

"Bloody rubbish, Bec. My phone went missing and was told her flight was delayed. It was not until I was already in flight when I learned what happened."

"You have got to be kidding me, man. Seriously, that is your lame excuse? I think I prefer the story of party boy out celebrating and taking two blondes back to his hotel room for the night."

"I am too knackered to play this game with you. Please just let me talk to her."

"If you think for one second about coming for her, I am making a promise now to stop you at every turn," I threaten as I hear E's bedroom door open, and she walks out. Meekly, she whispers, "Bec…can you…." Emelia immediately hits the floor, and I go racing to her, dropping my phone to check her out. "Emelia… o my god!" She has completely passed out, and now has blood dripping down the side of her head.

"Hello! Bec! What is going on?"

"Shit…" I hiss, picking my phone back up. "I have to go, Lucas, she just fainted."

Acknowledgements

Big thank you to my family and friends and those who loved my debut novel, giving me the encouragement to push forward. For being by my side as I navigate through the harsh reality of loss.

HUGE thank you to my editor, Jenni Gauntt. You are a brilliant rockstar in my eyes and can't wait to work with you on more stories!

Big Shout Out to Whitnay Edes for formatting the most gorgeous books. I fall in love with the pages even more every time I flip through them.

To my PA, Brandi Reyna for always keeping me in line, supportive words and for all the time you put into promoting and editing my books. Along with all the extras she does on the side.

To my TikTok girl, Olivia Matthews. For taking on this app that overwhelms me in every sense when it comes to reels and promoting. For being a wonderful soul that I am thankful to know.

Thank you to all my readers and friends who have supported me through this journey. Including my small town that includes my favorite bookstore, The Dragon's Lair Bookshop, owned by the most beautiful soul I have met, Shauna Cochran.

Thank you to all from the depths of my heart,

Ali Marie

If you enjoyed Heart Like a Truck, (even if not), I would appreciate it if you left an honest review.

Author Ali Marie

Alimarie_writelife

Author Ali Marie

Other Books by Ali Marie

Bluebonnet Days

Heart Like A Truck - A Novella